REAL GOOD MAN

Book One of the **REAL DUET**

MEGHAN MARCH

ABOUT THIS BOOK

We've had our fair share of bad boys. Now it's time for a *Real Good Man*. From *USA Today* best-selling author Meghan March comes a sexy new duet with a hero you won't want to miss.

Fall for a woman over text messages? No way in hell.

Reality can never be as good as the fantasy, right?

Wrong. It's better.

Banner Regent is smart, funny, and she's so far out of my league, she might as well be royalty.

I'm a mechanic from Kentucky. She's a New York City party girl.

We were never supposed to meet, but one text started something neither of us saw coming.

How do you seduce the woman who already has everything?

Show her what it's like to be with a real good man.

ONE

Banner

"IT'S NOT LIKE I SENT HIM A PIC OF MY AMAZING rack or something, so there's no need to get your granny panties in a twist, Frau Frances."

My neighbor from across the hall, who I'd guess is older than the gates of hell, covers her ears and closes her eyes like a toddler.

"Oh, that's really mature. Here I am trying to inject some color into your black-and-white-silent-movie-like old-lady existence, and you're going to ignore me? Nice. Really nice."

In all honesty, I don't give a damn that Myrna Frances doesn't want to hear about this texting-but-not-sexting relationship I have going on, because I've gotten to the point that I have to tell someone. My best friend is AWOL, and therefore I'm left with little choice but to spill here.

Actually, that's a lie. I would have tortured Myrna with it anyway just to get this very reaction out of her. I consider it my good deed of the day. Without my daily doses of color, she might die of boredom.

Our apartments each take up half of the next-to-the-top floor in our Manhattan building, and while I leave every day no matter what, even if it's just to replenish my vodka supply or go to work, she rarely makes it past the sidewalk into the outside world.

Myrna drops her hands from her ears and opens her eyes. The wrinkles around her mouth deepen when she scowls at me. "Why are you still here? And why won't you give me back my key, dammit?"

"Because your daughter asked me to check on you five years ago, and for some reason that I can't explain, I really enjoy that arching thing you do with your eyebrow when you pretend to be shocked by things I'm saying. Very Maleficent of you. You can admit it—you watch the movie and practice, don't you?"

Myrna's frown deepens to villainess levels at the mention of her daughter. "Ungrateful child. Never comes to visit. Too busy with her superficial life to even remember the woman who gave birth to her." This isn't the first time she's said it, or even the twentieth time.

"Yep, she's really superficial, what with being a member of Congress and all."

"I'm sure she slept her way to the top."

Ouch, Myrna is especially pissed today. I play along with her anyway, because at least this way I know she's getting her heart rate up. Being pissed off is about as close to cardio as she gets.

"You know, I'll have to check. Chances are she really did—with every man, woman, and tranny in her congressional district. She's going to need surgery to tighten up that cooch of hers."

"Get out!"

Myrna's tone has crossed into screech territory, but I can see she's fighting a smile. The old bat will eventually admit she loves how much I bother her. *Eventually.*

"Not until you open your present."

Our exchange of ridiculousness isn't going to be over until Myrna sees what I brought for her. I haven't given her a heart attack yet with one of my gifts, so I'm pretty sure she's not going to kick the bucket today.

Mumbling something to herself about the world going to hell if I'm an example of the quality of the generation left in charge, she tears open the pink paper (not noticing the even fainter pink penises on it, much to my disappointment), and flips the lid off the box.

"What in the hell is this?" She lifts the black-and-silver silicone phallus out of the box.

"You told me to eat a bag of dicks last time—good use of *Urban Dictionary*, by the way—so I brought you a big black cock. It even vibrates. I swear that thing can even get *you* off."

I'm not sure how to describe the sound that croaks from her old lady lips, but it turns into a shrill battle cry as she hurls the gorgeous faux phallus toward me. Jordana, Myrna's dog, bounds off her pink princess cushion and pounces in the direction of the vibrator.

"Are you trying to kill me with that thing?"

Myrna recoils as the dick rolls harmlessly across the floor as the Chinese crested hairless dog, clad in a green-and-pink argyle sweater, sniffs at it. Quite frankly, I'm impressed that the battery compartment didn't burst open.

Good to know it's durable.

3

I rise from the torture device Myrna calls a chair as Jordana gives the cock a lick.

"Jordana, don't you dare— Ugh, Banner! Get it away from her! She'll choke on—"

"A dick? That would be a sad way to go for Ms. Jordy." My words are sincere. Well, they are through my laughter.

I grab the vibrator off the floor before the dog can sink her toothless gums into the silicone, and toss it back onto Myrna's lap.

"All right, esteemed elder of the world. Have a lovely day plotting my death."

"Get out! And take this with you!"

"Nope. You need a good O more than I do. Same time tomorrow?"

She glares at me with such force, I'm a little shocked I'm not feeling the daggers shred my skin.

"Of course, you horrible child."

"That's what I thought." I give her a cheeky wave and a wink.

Sofia, Myrna's caretaker, emerges from the kitchen with afternoon tea service comprised of crustless watercress sandwiches, peppermint tea, and Fig Newtons as I head for the door. Nasty combination, but I nab a Newton off the tray anyway and pop it in my mouth.

"You better not be stealing my cookies," Myrna yells from the living room.

Sofia rolls her eyes. "Why do you both delight in torturing each other? It's a mystery of the universe I'll never quite understand."

Sofia's Eastern European accent clings to the words, despite how hard I know she's worked to lose it. The statuesque brunette looks like she stepped off a runway, but the twenty-two-year-old came from a much rougher beginning.

"Drinks tomorrow night?"

Sofia's eyes light up. "Yes, please."

"Good. Come over when you finish your shift. I should be home from work."

Before I can escape from the apartment, Myrna comes out from the living room, leaning heavily on her cane to impart one last bit of wisdom.

"You know what's wrong with your generation, Banner? You don't understand a damn thing about relationships. You're all texting this and sexting that. You don't actually meet people in person and talk to them. You hook up and sneak out. Men don't ask permission to call because they've already gotten what they wanted. You don't hold back and make them work for it."

"Are you calling me easy, Myrna?"

She shrugs a frail shoulder. "You said it, not me."

Her insight stings, but I keep my smile pinned in place.

"Enjoy the big black cock. It might just change your mind about how good it can be to get some dick."

She waves me off with a middle-finger salute, and I escape her pearls of wisdom and judgment.

Myrna is the crankiest old woman I've ever met, but for some reason, I love being around her. Her daughter and son-in-law drop in no more than three times a year, and the rest of the days she's left with paid caretakers like Sofia, who are kind but are still no substitute for family.

Basically, Myrna's exactly what I'm terrified my future is going to look like—old and alone with no one who gives a damn except the people who collect a paycheck from me.

At least her dog is loyal. If I weren't still one hundred percent selfish and could actually keep a goldfish alive, maybe I'd get one. *Nah. Too much commitment.*

Annnd we've just crossed into the depressing-as-shit *portion of the afternoon.*

My phone vibrates with a text as I jam my key into the lock on my apartment door. I freeze, excitement humming through me. I can't believe I've gotten sucked into this weird texting relationship with a man I've never met. But I can't stop.

I mean, I would have stopped, but then my investigative (okay, call them stalkerish) skills got the best of me, and I found his picture.

Wearing fatigues, a wifebeater, and combat boots, Logan Brantley looks like one of those pictures women post on Pinterest boards but know they'll never meet in real life unless it's possibly on the stage of some *Magic Mike* strip show. Except Logan is the real deal.

But we don't sext. We don't send naked pics. And there's no dirty talk. We've actually become *friends* in the last couple of weeks, and his texts fill some kind of need in my life I didn't know I had.

Manhattan's Queen of One-Night Stands, my self-proclaimed title, has suddenly fallen into a friendship with a guy who lives hundreds of miles away. And the more we text, the more I realize that maybe the men of New York I've been one-nighting aren't the most masculine specimens around.

Basically, every time I go on a date, I end up texting Logan the same question, but with multiple variations. *Would a real man . . .* and I'd fill in the blank.

Wear a rose-and-gray cashmere scarf?
Pair a bow tie with pressed jeans?
Order an elderflower martini?

I think it's safe to say that Logan Brantley's opinion of the men of Manhattan, at least the ones I've gone out with lately, is sinking faster than the Titanic.

I pull out my phone, anticipation zinging through me. That anticipation dies a quick death when the name on the screen isn't Logan's. Instead it's the guy I met on the sidewalk outside my office while waiting for my car service to pull up. No cashmere scarf, bow tie, or pressed jeans. So maybe he's a better bet?

I swipe and read the text.

> BRANDON SIDEWALK: *How about we grab a drink at 8? My friend's new bar is opening tomorrow, and he's having a preview tonight.*

My fingers are poised over the keyboard to say no. All I want right now is an amazing orgasm, and I already know I'm not going to get it from Brandon of the Sidewalk. I have a sense for these things.

But . . . maybe I could get my martini fix there. I am a sucker for the extra dirty.

> BANNER: *Where?*
> BRANDON SIDEWALK: *8th and 43rd. The bar is called Olivesque.*

I pull up Google and do some quick searching. There are a few articles about Olivesque's impending opening and lots of good things to say about it. Apparently Brandon Sidewalk has some fancy friends, because it's predicted that Olivesque will be impossible to get into for at least three or four months after it opens.

As a born-and-bred New Yorker with a taste for the exclusive, I can't say no.

I'm only going for the martini, I tell myself.

BANNER: I'll meet you there at 8.
BRANDON SIDEWALK: Great! Looking forward to it.

TWO

Banner

I'M THANKFUL THE SMELL OF SMOKE DOESN'T CLING TO my clothes as I let myself into my apartment. Oh, and that I escaped from overly friendly Brandon without letting him shove his hand up my skirt. I didn't see that coming. I figured he'd be overly polite, but instead he was pretty much a dick. Par for the Manhattan course, I suppose.

With the buzz of good vodka thrumming along with indignation through my veins, I pull out my phone.

> BANNER: *Would a real man try to feel up a woman in a bar when it's clear she's not interested and tells him to keep his hands to himself? Asking for a friend.*

I make a beeline for my bathroom and turn on the shower and the tub. First, I need to wash the film of grossness off me, and then I'm going to soak for an hour and take care of business. And by business, I mean I'm going to get that killer orgasm I've been dying for all day.

I'm already over halfway through my shower routine when my phone vibrates on the counter. If it's Brandon Sidewalk asking me to go out again, my reply will be epic.

I rinse the conditioner out of my hair and end my shower early. I tell myself it's only because I'm worried that the tub will run over if I don't check on the water level.

Riiight. It has nothing to do with the text waiting on my phone, and me hoping it's Logan. Nothing.

Hopping out, I don't bother toweling dry before I grab my phone off the counter.

LOGAN REAL MAN BRANTLEY: *Who do I need to kill?*

Should that alpha-caveman response send shivers through all the best parts of me? No, because we're just *friends*. But that doesn't change the fact that my nipples are hard and goose bumps rise along my arms.

BANNER: *I'll check with my friend.*
LOGAN REAL MAN BRANTLEY: *Cut the shit, Banner. No real man touches a woman when she says no.*
BANNER: *A real man would have her begging him instead, right? I know you would.*

I freeze a second after I hit SEND.
Crap. I officially crossed the line.
I hold my breath as I wait for a response. There are things I think about saying to Logan, especially when I picture him naked while I'm lying in bed, but I've been *so good* by not saying them to him over the phone. I told myself I wouldn't do this with him. I'd keep him in the safe zone so

I didn't screw everything up and lose whatever it is we have between us.

But I did it anyway because I suck.

I release my breath and carefully and deliberately lay my phone back on the counter and walk naked and dripping to my kitchen to pull a bottle of vodka out of the freezer. I dump two fingers into a glass and toss in a couple of ice cubes before calmly making my way back to the bathroom and my steaming tub.

What if he doesn't answer?

What if he never texts me back again?

Then I'll drink more vodka and mourn the loss of this ridiculous connection to a man I've never met.

What's my fascination with him, anyway? The answers come in rapid-fire succession.

He's blunt and to the point, and never bullshits me when I ask him a question. He's nothing like the men of Manhattan who I date. He's safe and from a completely different world seven hundred miles away, and I figured there was no way I could screw this up by sleeping with him.

Isn't that enlightening?

The tail end of a vibration trails off as I walk back into my bathroom, and my heartbeat immediately kicks up.

I snatch my phone off the counter.

> LOGAN REAL MAN BRANTLEY: *If she's not begging, he's doing something wrong. Ladies always come first. I want a name.*

My hand shakes as I carry the phone and my drink to the tub, and position both on the edge as I slide into the

11

steaming water.

After dabbing my wet fingers on the towel rolled up in a basket to my left, I tap out my reply.

BANNER: Brandon Sidewalk, never to be repeated.

I flip my phone facedown on the ledge around the tub and sink into the water.

Logan could definitely make me beg. Jesus, this is the worst idea I've ever had. What made me think I could keep from ruining this?

When I first got a text from Logan Brantley's number, it was really coming from my best friend, Greer, who'd been without her phone due to some really crazy shit. Greer, being the awesome friend she is, found a Good Samaritan who let her use his phone to text me so I'd stop losing my freaking mind.

But instead of getting Greer when I texted back, I got the Good Samaritan—Logan Brantley, former US marine, one hundred percent Kentucky redneck, and the opposite of every man I've ever met. Once I finished my online stalking and saw his picture, is it any surprise I kept texting him?

I reach below the surface of the water, wishing I'd grabbed a toy to aid the *Get Banner to Orgasm Really, Really Fast* cause, but I can do the job without any assistance.

Adjusting into a more comfortable position, I let my legs fall to the sides of the tub. Pleasure buzzes through my veins as I picture the forbidden: Logan on top of me, pounding into me over and over.

My phone vibrates from the ledge. I shake off the water

and once again blot my fingers on a towel.

> LOGAN REAL MAN BRANTLEY: *I'll be there on Friday. Brandon Sidewalk better have a real name by the time I get there.*

My pounding heart kicks up, thudding with a jacked-up rhythm as my phone slips from my fingers and tumbles to the floor, sliding across the travertine tiles and out of reach. Motionless in the tub, I stare at it as I freak the hell out.

No. Not possible. Logan has no reason to be in New York. He's kidding. It's fine. My fantasy isn't going to come to life only to be shattered as soon as I meet him. Nothing is going to happen. I can keep him in the safe zone. No more dirty texts. Just dirty thoughts. It's fine.

I stay in the water until it cools down, no orgasm in sight, because my brain won't stop spinning with the possibilities.

He has to be joking. There's no possible way that Logan Brantley of Gold Haven, Kentucky, is coming to New York. Nothing to worry about here.

When I finally climb out of the tub and wrap myself in a fluffy towel, I take measured steps across the floor to retrieve my phone. My hand isn't shaking when I pick it up, or so I tell myself.

With the rampaging beat of my heart nearing life-threatening levels, I stare down at the screen as it comes to life.

> LOGAN REAL MAN BRANTLEY: *What's your address?*

Holy. Shit.

THREE

Logan

I TAKE A SWIG OF MY BUD, GRAB MY WRENCH, AND LEAN over the engine of the car I'm working on. My grip flexes hard against the steel at the thought some guy would dare touch a woman without her consent. What the fuck is wrong with those New Yorker assholes? It's not how I planned to tell Banner I was going to be in town, but fuck if that woman doesn't get me all kinds of tied up.

Banner.

What the hell kind of name is that for a woman, anyway?

After one encounter with her friend Greer, I know exactly what kind of woman she has to be—the kind who's so far out of my league, I shouldn't even be thinking about her.

And yet here I am spending time I need to be using to turn cars into cash, texting with her.

If you asked me a month ago, I would have laughed my ass off at the idea that I'd get into something with a woman I've never met in person. I've never even thought about trying the disaster of online dating. But somehow I ended up sucked into something I'm not sure how to explain, with a woman living hundreds of miles away.

But dammit, I'm intrigued by her. Her *would a real man* questions never fail to make me laugh. What the hell kind of men are living up there? Jesus fucking Christ. These douche bags make it stupid easy to make fun of them.

Then again, the same guys would look at me and see a former jarhead, lifelong redneck, and now professional grease monkey trying to carve out a living in a one-stop-light town. Those Wall Street types wouldn't even shake my hand. *Fuck 'em.*

So, why am I hauling my ass all the way to New York to deliver the Road Runner instead of turning it over to a car hauler?

Because I have to meet her. I need to find out once and for all that she's not really as funny and cute as she comes across over these damn texts. The best way to ruin a fantasy is to meet the reality, right? I'm sure she'll take one look at me and turn up her nose.

But what if she doesn't?

The fact that she hasn't answered my text yet isn't sitting right with me. That's all fine and good because a real man isn't afraid to fight for what he wants—and what I want is to cure myself of this fascination.

At least, that's what I'm telling myself. If I were to admit the truth, it's that her messages seem to pull a smile from me every time, even when I'm staring down the deadline from hell like I have been on this rebuild. Somehow, whatever we have going on reminds me that there's more to life than making a dollar.

I toss the wrench aside and grab a rag off my workbench

to wipe my hands. I'm done for tonight.

Over the earsplitting sound of Metallica, someone pounds on the garage door.

What the hell?

It's quarter after ten, and this whole sleepy town is tucked in except for the diehards drinking at the bowling alley for Wednesday night league. The only reason I'm up is to hit this ridiculous fucking deadline so I can load the car on a trailer tomorrow and collect the rest of my cash.

I stride to the service door, flip the lock, and pull it open.

"Damn, Logan. What's a girl gotta do to get your attention these days?" Julianne Liefer stands at the door with a fifth of Wild Turkey and a bucket of a fried chicken from Cluck You.

"Did you need something?" I ask as the wafting scent of grease hits my nose.

"Thought you might need some dinner. I just finished a super-fucking-long appointment turning a client's hair into a friggin' masterpiece, and she had her husband drop me off some fried chicken and booze when he picked her up. I saw your truck, so I figured I'd offer to share. There's potato wedges, biscuits, and slaw too."

Julianne's salon sits right across from my repair shop, and we've fallen into an easy friendship. The people of Gold Haven jokingly refer to her salon as Cut a Bitch, rather than the real name, Cut It Best. Cut a Bitch is more accurate when it comes to how she treats the people who piss her off.

Julianne recently broke it off with my buddy Granger, and I'm really fucking hoping she hasn't decided I'd make a hell of a rebound.

There's no way I'd go there, even if she isn't like most of the women in this town—just looking for a man to take care of them. Julianne works her ass off as hard as I do.

"I already had some dinner."

She gives me a look that says *oh really?* "A Hot Pocket doesn't count as real food." She slides by me, the bucket of chicken crushing around the edges between us.

"You're bound to get grease all over yourself if you're not careful."

She looks back and winks at me. "A little grease isn't gonna hurt a real woman. I like getting dirty."

Banner's blunt message comes back to me. *A real man would have her begging him instead, right? I know you would.*

She called it right, because there was nothing I like more than a woman at my mercy, begging for relief.

I glance at where my phone waits in my toolbox, and wonder if Banner has responded with her address or if she's gonna chicken out on me.

I don't have time to think about it for long because Julianne drops the bucket of chicken on the workbench and pulls two stools together. She twists the top off the Wild Turkey and takes a swig before holding it out to me.

"Today has been for shit. One of my stylists got into it with my nail tech and they both walked out, leaving me to deal with the mess of appointments they had scheduled. I could've gone home and eaten my fried chicken alone on my couch, but that would put me in an even worse mood than I'm in now, so just fucking humor me, Logan."

I take the bottle from her and twist the cap back on before grabbing a piece of chicken from the bucket.

"At least you don't have to worry that I'm using food

to try to trap you into a ring like Emmy Harris. I just want some company."

I almost choke on my first bite of chicken at the mention of Emmy Harris, the manager of Home Cookin' who brings apple dumplings and peach pie to the shop on what seems like a regular basis. It started out innocently about nine months ago when I got so frigging busy I didn't have time to go home and cook for myself, and ended up at Home Cookin' damn near every day of the week.

Emmy talked me into taking her to the movies a couple of times, and dinner somewhere other than Home Cookin' once, but when she started dropping hints about wanting to see each other exclusively and talking about how the house she's building would be great for a family, I backed off. I thought we were friends, but she seems to have developed different ideas. It helps that I've been too busy to go on a date anyway, so my excuses to her haven't been complete BS.

Especially since I'd rather work my ass off and take random breaks to text a woman I've never met.

Yeah, I've got no explanation for that.

The more I think about it as I pack away the greasy chicken, I decide there's something seriously wrong with me. I've got flesh-and-blood women in Gold Haven who understand exactly the kind of man I am, but instead here I am getting ready to drive to New York because I need to satisfy my curiosity about Banner. She's from a totally different world, and we're not going to have a damn thing in common, but even that knowledge isn't stopping me from doing it.

Julianne knocks back another shot of Wild Turkey, not

expecting or waiting for a reply from me, which is smart. I don't have a whole lot to say when my thoughts are all twisted around Banner.

Why am I pushing this with her?

Because there's something about her I can't get out of my mind.

One trip. One meeting. That's all I need, and I'll know exactly how ridiculous this has been from the beginning.

My phone buzzes from its spot in the open lid of my toolbox, and both Julianne and I look toward it.

"Someone who's going to be jealous that I'm sitting here?"

Would Banner be jealous? I have no fucking clue. I wipe my hands and reach for it.

Instead of the address I asked for, I get a different message.

BANNER NYC: Are you serious?

I give her the truth.

LOGAN: Yes. Friday. It's time we meet in person.

I wait for a moment, but when her reply doesn't come right away, I put the phone back in its place and respond to Julianne.

"A friend."

"Does she know she makes you light up like that? Or that she's a lucky bitch because of it?"

"She's not up for discussion."

Julianne whistles as she grabs for another piece of

chicken. "Does Emmy know about her competition?"

"This isn't any of Emmy's business."

Julianne raises an eyebrow. "So . . . who is the mystery woman? Do I know her?"

Finally, I snag the bottle of Wild Turkey, uncap it, and dump some in the empty coffee mug that's still sitting unwashed from my last fill-up this afternoon. "No."

"Fine; be difficult. I'm sure I'll find out one way or another." She pauses, and the shit-stirrer in her comes to life. "You tell her you're with another woman right now?"

I give her a hard look. If I'm not careful, Julianne will spread my business all over town. She's the queen of the gossip grapevine, and I don't need any part of it.

"There's nothing to tell. You said it yourself—this was a better alternative than going home by yourself and realizing you just broke up with the best thing that ever happened to you."

Julianne's shoulders stiffen. "Granger Ryan wasn't the best thing that ever happened to me. I was the best thing that ever happened to him. He just couldn't get his head out of his ass long enough to appreciate what he had, so he lost it."

My friend Granger, the fire chief in this small town, is still pissed about how she marched into the station and told him it was over—in front of all his volunteer firemen.

Either way, the subject of who is texting me closes.

Now, I just gotta get Banner's address so I can track her down as soon as this Road Runner is in the hands of its owner.

FOUR

Banner

I DRAG SOFIA INTO MY APARTMENT WHEN SHE KNOCKS on the door Thursday evening. This is the absolute worst time not to have my best girlfriend around to spill to, but I have to tell someone.

"I apologize in advance, but you have to listen to everything I say and tell me what to do." *Because clearly I can't be trusted to make rational decisions about this man*, I add silently.

"What's going on?" Sofia's accent is thicker than normal in her confusion.

"You remember the guy I've been texting with?"

"The one you've been torturing Mrs. Frances with for weeks?"

"I might dispute the use of the word *torture*, but yes. Him. He's coming here. Tomorrow."

"Here? New York, here?"

"Yes. Here. New York. Manhattan. And I don't know what to do. Help."

Rarely do I ever have my confidence totally knocked

off its axis, but this situation is an anomaly. Logan is supposed to stay inside my little magic box of a phone where I feel like I'm still in control, because the second he becomes real, as in flesh and blood, all bets are off.

"You have to meet him. I mean, you can't miss this chance."

"I can't! I'm going to screw everything up, and then—" I cut myself off before I can admit that it's going to suck so much major donkey dick if I lose him in my life. Even in this short period of time, I've gotten attached to whatever we have.

"And then what? What could you possibly screw up? It's not like you're planning to marry the guy or something, right?"

Sofia's question stops me cold and tosses me years into the past. I mumble a response as I head for the kitchen and my trusty bottle of vodka in the freezer. Sofia's Russian, I think, so she can hack it.

Someday, I'm going to be able to face the idea of marriage without thinking of Livingston Armstrong's mother telling him that I'm the kind of girl you bang in a frat house, not the kind of girl you bring to the Hamptons to meet the family.

I should have known with a name like Livingston, he'd be a pretentious douche bag.

The rest of the memory replays in my head like it happened yesterday.

"But she's from a great family, Mother."

Haughty Mrs. Armstrong didn't care. "She might be from a good family, but that doesn't mean she's cut from the same cloth. That girl is trouble. Mark my words. Sow your wild oats with that one, and then go find a nice girl to settle down with. Her mother must be so ashamed to have such a brash and classless daughter. Don't ever bring her back here."

Livingston dropped his gaze to his lap as his mother looked up and caught me watching them from around the corner. She didn't take back a single word or apologize. No, instead she tilted her head and raised a brow.

Bitch.

Livingston didn't get to sow any more wild oats with me. I told the entire female Greek population at Amherst that his dick was too small to be bothered with, and he had to find girls from other schools to date until graduation.

That was the last time I let myself think about my future in terms of a single guy.

I'm not the marrying type, and while I fought not to take Mrs. Armstrong's words to heart, she gutted me with one sentence of solid truth. My mother was ashamed, not only about me being brash and classless, but also about the fact that I refused to go to MIT and follow in my parents' footsteps.

I ended up at Amherst, much to their disappointment, and they essentially washed their hands of me after that. So instead of becoming a studious little future scientist, I became something else entirely—the life of the party with no intention of ever settling down.

"Banner? Are you listening to me?"

I turn around with the vodka bottle in hand and shake myself free of the past. "Sorry, spaced out. What did you say?"

"Are you worried he's not going to like you? I'm not sure that's possible. Men love you. All of them."

"Men love my tits, ass, and dirty mouth," I reply, my tone flippant. My pride won't let me admit that I'm terrified Logan Brantley won't like the rest of me.

I'm being ridiculous. Screw him if he doesn't like me. I'm awesome.

I remind myself I don't care what anyone thinks, let alone some guy I'll probably never see again. *Why am I freaking out about this, anyway?*

Taking a swig straight from the bottle, I focus on the smooth burn of the vodka sliding down my throat and announce, "We're going out."

Sofia throws both hands into the air, and I know she needs tonight as badly as I do. "Can I change in your bathroom? I didn't want Mrs. Frances to see me get slutted up. Her words, not mine."

I smile. "Yes, definitely. Get on with your slutty self."

She giggles like the twenty-two-year-old girl it's easy to forget she is, and pauses before turning toward the bathroom. "My skirt is so short, we won't pay for drinks all night. It might not solve your question about the guy, but it couldn't hurt."

"I'll worry about him tomorrow."

FIVE

Logan

I still haven't gotten an address from Banner as I load up the Road Runner to head out before the sun rises tomorrow morning. I have half a mind to pull some strings and figure out where she lives on my own if she doesn't respond. I'm not going to waste this chance just because she's suddenly having cold feet. Besides, that's not the woman I've gotten to know. She takes life head-on.

By the time I crank down the last ratchet strap, I decide I'm not gonna let her chicken out. Even without her address, I'm gonna meet Banner and satisfy my raging curiosity. Regardless of whatever else does or doesn't happen, the least I can do is show her how a real man treats a woman.

As though I conjured it through my thoughts, my phone buzzes with a text message.

I pull it out, and a smile tugs at the corner of my mouth.

It's an address. A second message comes through immediately after.

Banner NYC: We're not meeting at my place.

I type my reply.

LOGAN: *You don't trust me.*
BANNER NYC: *Maybe it's me I don't trust.*

Well now, isn't that an unexpected development.

LOGAN: *Maybe I'm hunchbacked with one eye and tiny T. rex hands.*
BANNER NYC: *Impossible. I've seen your picture.*
LOGAN: *How?*

There's no way Greer could have sent her one because she was using my phone, and I read the message she sent Banner. So when an old photo from my days in the corps appears on the screen of my phone, I'm more than a little surprised.

LOGAN: *You stalking me?*
BANNER NYC: *Have you changed much since then?*
LOGAN: *I don't carry an M16 everywhere.*
BANNER NYC: *No, but I bet you're packing below the belt. At least, that's what I assume . . .*
BANNER NYC: *I didn't mean to say that. I'm drunk. Ignore everything.*

Now, shit's getting interesting. I've been careful to keep my messages to her on the friendly side of the scale, but Banner has hinted at more now twice. It's time to stop with the games and put it out there for real.

LOGAN: *You imagining me naked?*

SIX

Banner

"**I** THINK I JUST MADE A TERRIBLE MISTAKE."

As Sofia returns to the table from the bathroom, her sleek brown eyebrows knit together. "What do you mean?" She looks down at the empty cocktail glasses between us. "And what happened to my drink?"

"I drank it. This was an emergency." I hold up my phone. "I basically told him I think about him naked."

Sofia's blue eyes widen as she stares at me. "I thought you said no drunk texting?"

I shrug and peer down into the empty glass. "You left me without adult supervision."

She slides into the chair at our tall cocktail table and laughs. "You're the adult here, Banner. You're how much older than me? And why does it matter, anyway? You're the queen of dirty texts."

"You seriously can't be asking me to do math right now, and it matters because I wasn't doing this with him. I was trying the friends thing."

Sofia looks at me like I'm not speaking English. "I don't

understand."

I trace the rim of the glass with my index finger, hesitating before I speak. "I'm basically good at three things when it comes to guys. Talking dirty, one-night stands, and the walk of shame. And then there's Logan. He's the first one in forever who talked to me without doing it just to fuck me. He has never asked me to send him a pic of my tits. He actually *likes* me, and without knowing if I look like Cruella de Vil. He's . . . different. So I thought that meant whatever he and I are doing would be different. But I couldn't help myself. I had to screw it all up."

I look toward the bar rather than make eye contact with Sofia, but my gaze snaps back to her when she asks, "Does he have a brother? I could use some *different* too."

"We haven't gotten that far. Maybe we never will. Ugh, I suck at this."

Sofia points to my phone where it rests on the table between us. "Are you going to answer him?"

"I have to, don't I?"

"He's coming here tomorrow?"

"Yes."

"And where are you going to meet him?"

"I gave him the address of the tapas bar on the corner."

"Really?"

Her question makes me reconsider my choice. "Bad idea?"

Sofia shrugs. "If he's so different, maybe tapas isn't your best choice. You'll find out tomorrow, I suppose. I need another drink, and I'm not waiting for the slow-as-hell waitress. Don't do anything ridiculous while I'm gone."

"Of course not," I say, my tone indignant.

I tap my phone screen as soon as Sofia struts away, and stare down at the message from Logan.

LOGAN REAL MAN BRANTLEY: You imagining me naked?

I'm so screwed, because I'm definitely picturing him naked *now*. All my resolutions about how this is supposed to be different don't stop my thumbs from flying across my screen with the absolute alcohol-induced truth. I've already messed this up. *And at least I'm being honest.*

BANNER: Only when I come.

His reply arrives within moments.

LOGAN REAL MAN BRANTLEY: Fuck. You shouldn't have told me that, because now I'm thinking about you too.
BANNER: Is that a bad thing?
LOGAN REAL MAN BRANTLEY: You tell me.

Oh. Well. Hmmm.

BANNER: I guess we'll find out when you get here.

As soon as I hit SEND and read back over the messages, a wave of excitement washes over me that I finally get to meet him in person, but there's a pang of regret with it. What are the chances I can break my old habits with him, and not end this with the walk of shame?

LOGAN REAL MAN BRANTLEY: I guess we will.

Now, what does that mean? Did he just shoot me down? *Gah, this man has me all over the place.*

I pause, my thumbs poised above the keyboard on my phone, unsure how to reply.

Sofia returns, no doubt saving me from messing this up even further by saying something more. "Hey! I ran into a friend. She's doing shots at the bar."

"Shots? I could do shots." My voice sounds unusually perky, even to me.

As we head over to join Sofia's friend, I decide more alcohol is the perfect way to help me figure out how to deal with Logan tomorrow . . . *although it might not be the smartest.*

I wake up in my own bed, but I'm not alone. Thankfully, the dark head on the pillow next to me belongs to Sofia. I vaguely recall her ushering us into a cab around three in the morning.

Thank God for the weekend, or I would be calling into work hung over again, which would probably result in me getting fired. And somehow that doesn't sound like the worst thing in the world, except for the fact that I'd be broke for the time being.

No, I can't lose this job. I have to stick it out for another six months, and then I'll be all set.

I roll and swing my legs over the side of the bed, taking my time as I stand to make sure I'm not going to land on my face. Balance acquired, I shuffle into the bathroom to find my clutch on the counter.

Out of habit more than anything else, I flip it open and pull out my phone. Two texts from Logan are waiting.

That familiar rush of excitement floods me when I see his name on the screen. Rather than unlocking my phone to read them, I force myself into the shower to rid myself of the smoke and club nastiness from last night. My hair looks like it's been styled by a two-year-old, and my eyeliner smudges should qualify me for honorary raccoon status.

The steam from the shower melts it all away, and thankfully my stomach isn't angry with me for whatever I put in it. I hurry through sudsing up, washing, and conditioning because I need to know what Logan said. Even now, he's somewhere between Kentucky and Manhattan. Equal parts anticipation and apprehension battle it out in my chest.

I like this guy.

That's the terrifying part. I don't know what his cock looks like, or his favorite position in bed, but I *like him* as a person. That's not something I've been able to say in a long time.

It's not like Logan and his messages have been part of my life for long, so how did both become so important so fast?

Tonight can't be the end.

I will not one-night him.

Resolute in my decision, I shut the water off and reach for my towel. Feeling confident about my newfound determination, I unlock my phone and the messages appear on the screen.

LOGAN REAL MAN BRANTLEY: *Those are things I'd*

rather discuss in person.

Logan Real Man Brantley: Get some sleep, Banner. You're going to need it.

Oh God. What did I say? After the shots, I thought I told Sofia to take my phone away. I scroll upward through the messages I sent him.

Banner: So, anal . . . I need to see the equipment 1st. 2 big is a thing.

My stomach twists and plummets to my feet.

Sofia didn't take my phone from me. Jesus Christ. This is a train wreck.

Above that, I asked him if he was cut or uncut. Whether he liked his balls played with while he got head. If he would pull my hair.

I glance up and see myself in the mirror. All the color has drained from my face, and I'm doing a great impersonation of a drowned albino rat. That is, if albino rats had fabulous colorists.

My gaze drops back to the phone as I read the rest of the damage. Logan deflected all my questions, but he wasn't rude or unkind.

How am I ever going to face him after all that? What must he think of me?

My stomach still twisting, I wander into my living room and curl up on the couch under my fuzziest blanket.

If I was worried about screwing it up before . . . mission accomplished. Is this my own form of self-sabotage? Maybe I'm so scared that I actually like Logan, that I want to make sure there's no possible way this could actually go well?

This is what happens when you know you need a shrink but refuse to go to one. You psychoanalyze yourself and do a really crappy job at it.

I need a voice of reason. I need Greer, but I can't talk to her because she's way too busy sorting out her own life right now.

Grabbing a throw pillow, I squish it over my head and groan.

SEVEN

Logan

THE DRIVE TO NEW YORK IS A LONG ONE AND GIVES me way too much time to think. What the fuck am I doing?

I wish Banner hadn't caught my attention the way she has, but how could she not? Smart, sarcastic, confident, and funny as hell. She isn't looking for a man to take care of her, because she has the world at her fingertips.

So, what can a guy like me possibly offer a woman who has everything? From the turn our messages took last night, it's clear I have at least one thing to offer her.

She might have been drunk, but that's when a lot of the truth comes out. I wish I could be a fly on the wall when she reads the messages this morning. Banner didn't just cross the line. She obliterated it.

I'm not pissed about that, but until I meet her in person, I'm withholding judgment.

My goal for tonight? To have an amazing fucking time with her, regardless of whether we end up naked or not. And if we do, you better believe I'm going to leave her measuring every guy she's ever been with against me. That's what a real man does.

Banner has been radio silent all day, and I'm starting to wonder if she changed her mind. Would it surprise me? Hell yes. Would I let it stand? No way in hell. If she isn't interested in anything beyond a drink and a meal, that's her call. But there's no way I'm going to let her chicken out before I get to introduce myself face-to-face.

Decision made, I turn my attention to the road where it belongs.

EIGHT

Banner

AFTER SOFIA LEFT TO GO HOME, I CHANGED MY outfit fourteen times, and now it looks like Fifth Avenue threw up all over my bedroom.

What do you wear when you're trying to prove that you're not cheap and easy despite your text messages while you were drunk the night before? I'm coming up blank. Six dresses, two pairs of jeans, four skirts, two jumpsuits (what was I thinking when I bought those, anyway?), and countless tanks, shirts, blouses, and sweaters lay strewn across every flat and not-so-flat surface in my bedroom.

Do I go casual? Sexy? Flirty? Boring?

Once again, I wish Greer were here so she could stage a fashion intervention. *What would Greer wear?*

My best friend is classy to the nth degree, so she'd probably go with one of the more conservative dresses. Or possibly a skirt-and-blouse combo.

But then again, I'm not Greer.

I look down at the dresses on my bed and close my eyes.

"Eeny, meeny, miney, mo." I reach out and grab a handful of fabric and decide that whatever it is, I'm going to wear it. I have approximately thirty minutes to finish getting ready, so I need to hurry my ass up.

I open my eyes and look down at what I picked.

A long-sleeved, olive-drab shirt dress with gold buttons and a matching belt. I pulled it out of my closet on a whim while picturing Logan in his uniform.

Do I really want to wear *that*? It's probably the least sexy of everything I've picked, but maybe that's exactly why it's perfect.

Because I'm not going to have sex with Logan Brantley.

I pull it on over plain black lingerie, not even the lacy kind, before straightening everything and tying the belt. I look . . . conservative. It's like the anti-Banner.

I tell myself unfastening the top button makes it look a little more Banner-ish, but still conservative. Not like when I unfastened the top three buttons while trying it on in the store so the neckline played peekaboo with my bra.

Classic gold accessories complete the look, and my hair is curled in waves down my back. I slip into my favorite knee-high black boots and pull on a black trench coat.

I look very New York.

My reflection hammers home the fact that the guy I'm meeting is the complete opposite of everything New York, which is exactly why I'm so freaking fascinated by him.

Except now I'm not sure I'm going to be able to look him in the eye after the downward spiral my texts took last night. With any other guy, sending flirty or downright dirty messages wouldn't bother me. That's who I am—the girl who isn't afraid to say all those filthy things and follow through on them. But for some reason, what Logan thinks of me actually matters, and I don't want him to put me in that category.

Then why did I do it?

Because I'm an idiot who shouldn't be let near a bottle of vodka without adult supervision.

I'm not going for shock value here, which means I'm completely out of my depth. I've never wanted to impress someone by just being myself before.

For the love of God, I need to stop with the introspection.

I have to get out of my head, so I clean up my clothing disaster and make sure my bed is made. *Why am I bothering? We aren't sleeping together.* Still, I take the time to look over everything again before glancing at the clock.

It's go time.

Why did I pick this place? When I walk into the tapas bar, I question that decision and every other one I've made in my life since I got that first text message from Logan Brantley's number. He isn't a tapas kind of guy. He's steak and potatoes and *man food*. Or even bar food. Anything but tapas.

I'm castigating myself for being an absolute moron and not thinking this through as I allow the hostess to lead me to a table in the front corner where I'll have a view of the door. I check my phone and the time every thirty seconds.

When it vibrates, I freeze.

SOFIA: *Good luck tonight. Mrs. F says to keep your legs closed.*

At least that brings a smile to my face. And it's probably some of the best advice I've ever gotten. *Thanks, Frau Frances.*

Tonight I'm determined not to let my normal throw-caution-to-the-wind attitude have free rein, because every time I do, I fall into my same old habits. I'm not doing that with Logan. *No, really. I'm not.*

The door opens and I hold my breath.

Not him.

It opens again and again over the next fourteen minutes, and none of the people who come inside look anything like the guy in the picture I've been getting off to nearly every night for the last couple of weeks.

Finally, fifteen minutes after we said we'd meet, Logan Brantley walks into the tapas bar. Every curse word known to woman—and several I make up on the fly—flash through my brain.

This isn't fair. Logan Brantley is even sexier when he's not dressed in camo and carrying a big gun. More than one head swings in his direction. Women flip their hair and un-cross and re-cross their legs as he steps up to the hostess stand.

A shaft of possessiveness lights up inside me, right along with nervous energy and my pounding heart. *Back off, bitches. He's not here for you.*

I hear the low rumble of his deep drawl when he speaks to the hostess. She gestures in my direction, and he turns. Piercing blue eyes find me at the table where a lone water glass sits in front of me.

Liquid courage should definitely have been on the menu. Why didn't I order a drink?

Because I'm an idiot. Because I thought I could handle this.

Now my heart is hammering so loud, my voice will probably be inaudible, or even worse—quaver when I speak.

Logan walks toward me with long, sure strides. He's taller than I realized. And broader. And *bigger.* Everywhere. He's wearing a black Henley that stretches across his chest, leaving no doubt of the fact that the man is built. And his jeans. Jesus. They're worn and snug in all the right places.

The picture I found was clearly not recent, and it's not just the fact that his brown hair is longer and shaggier. He's one of those men who age *well.*

Logan stops in front of me when he reaches the tall bar table. He says nothing as his gaze drops to the toes of my boots and drags up every inch of my body.

"You're a hard woman to find."

His accent is absolutely delicious. The deep timbre reaches all the way to the very core of me, and I find myself uncrossing and re-crossing my legs just like the rest of the women in this bar.

"I gave you the address." I shoot for casual, and thankfully my voice doesn't shake.

"And for a guy with a dually truck and a trailer that had to park God knows where, that address was a challenge."

I swear I feel all the blood drain from my face. "Oh crap. I'm so sorry. I didn't even think—"

"Doesn't matter. I'm here. You're here." He holds out his hand. "Logan Brantley. It's nice to finally meet you in person, Ms. Banner . . ."

It hits me that through all of our texts, I never told him

my last name. "Regent." I slide my hand into his as he closes his wide fingers around it.

"Banner Regent," he says slowly, trying out my name.

My non-sexy black panties are never going to survive the way it rolls off his tongue in that drawl. All the dirty things I texted him last night are front and center in my mind and my girly parts.

No. I throw up a mental stop sign.

While my brain is being pulled in opposite directions, Logan is waiting for me to reply.

"You're going to hate tapas," I blurt out.

"I don't even know what tapas is."

"We should get out of here."

He raises one dark eyebrow. "And go where?"

My knee-jerk reaction is to take him home and fuck the living hell out of what might be the very first *real man* I've ever met. But that's not happening.

Keep your legs closed, Banner.

"Have you ever been to Times Square?"

He shakes his head. "No. Never been to New York before today."

I smile as I come up with the perfect way to keep myself out of bed with Logan Brantley.

"Then we better make it memorable."

NINE

Banner

ISN'T IT STRANGE HOW WHEN YOU LIVE IN A TOURISTY place, you don't do any of the touristy things until someone comes to visit from out of town? I've always been a New Yorker, so unless there's some specific reason to be there, I avoid Times Square like the plague.

But not tonight.

Tonight I need to be farther away from my apartment than this tapas bar, and I need to get whatever is between Logan and me under control before I give in to the urge to climb him. *Bad Banner.*

He might think this is a dumb idea, but I can't think of a less likely place for me to jump this incredibly sexy man's bones than a giant arcade.

I flag down a cab, and Logan opens the yellow door. I give directions to the cabbie as I slide in.

When Logan climbs inside next to me, the back of the taxi shrinks. Not only is Logan Brantley bigger than most guys I've shared the back of a cab with, there's something else. It goes beyond size to *presence*. Logan Brantley has it in spades, and I'm squeezing my thighs together in an effort to kill the ache that's building there.

I have to start talking, or God knows what I'll let myself do.

"This might seem unorthodox and probably not what you were expecting, but instead of trying to get into a fancy steak house and waiting hours for a table where you could actually get man food, I made an executive decision to do something completely different."

He's watching me as I ramble, and that intense blue gaze isn't helping me sound coherent.

"What did you have in mind?"

"There's a huge sports bar arcade in Times Square, and I thought it would be fun."

He nods, his eyes never leaving mine. "I can handle that." He pauses for a beat. "You don't seem like the sports bar or arcade type, though."

It's a fair observation, especially since he's right.

"I've been to plenty of sports bars," I tell him. "I am a New Yorker, after all, so I've got the Mets, Yankees, Giants, Knicks, and Rangers to cheer on."

"You like to watch sports?" His tone is more than a little surprised.

It's the moment of truth. Do I lie and pretend I'm some kind of real sports fan? Or do I just admit that I only go with friends when we're drinking and I ignore the game? I've never lied to impress a guy before, and I'm not going to start now.

"Unless someone gets a box at a game, I don't actually watch any sport. I go for the atmosphere."

"Fair enough. I don't usually have time, but I'll try to

catch a game on TV once in a while."

As expected, the cabbie gets stuck in traffic when heading down Seventh Avenue, but Logan keeps the conversation going.

"What about an arcade? I can't exactly picture you playing video games."

I respond with a shake of my head before elaborating. "Never in my life. But I can play a decent game of pool, and a marginally passable game of foosball."

"So this will be an experience for both of us then." His smile tilts into a smirk. "Might have to make a bet on a game of foosball. I'm more than passable myself."

I like the hint of challenge his words carry, and give him a sassy look of my own in return. "Oh, you're going to get cocky now? Just wait."

The cabbie interrupts from the front. "You wanna get out here? It'll be faster to walk in this mess."

"Sure, that's fine." I slide a twenty through the glass while Logan is still reaching for his wallet. He opens his mouth to protest, but I wave it off. "You can buy the first tokens."

He nods. "I'll be buying all the tokens."

Logan's hand closes around mine as he helps me climb out of the cab. He releases his hold when I step onto the sidewalk, but I feel it again on the small of my back as we make our way toward the entrance.

The Kentucky redneck is a gentleman. That shouldn't turn me on, but it does. I shut my thoughts down as he pauses to scan the buildings behind us.

"It really looks just like what you see on TV. All the lights. Huge buildings. Cool for a vacation, but I don't know how people get used to living in the middle of all of this."

I turn and take it in through his eyes. Everything is bigger, brighter, and louder in New York. I can only imagine how chaotic it must seem to someone who isn't used to it. Maybe about like the way Logan's presence is making me feel.

"I guess when you've lived here all your life, you don't know any different, though," he adds, his observation accurate.

"Pretty much. When I was a kid, I would beg my driver to take the route through Times Square. It was a treat to see all the lights since he normally avoided it."

"Your driver?"

When Logan's gaze lands on me, I still. I don't talk about my childhood much to anyone. It just slipped out.

I take a step toward the door. "My parents weren't around much when I was growing up, and they definitely don't drive. So, yeah, I had a driver as a kid."

Logan's expression is thoughtful, almost amused. "We really are from two different worlds. I pedaled my ass off three miles to school when I missed the bus. When I blew a tube, I walked."

"Your parents didn't take you?"

Logan shakes his head. "My ma worked graveyard, so she wasn't awake until after I got home from school, if she was even there."

"So basically we were both kids who raised ourselves because our parents were busy doing other things?"

Even though our circumstances were vastly different, it seems that Logan Brantley and I have more common ground than either of us realized.

The heat from his hand burns through my dress as he brings me closer to his side to miss a crowd of tourists snapping pictures and not paying attention to where they're walking.

I look up to find those blue eyes fixed on my face.

"I guess you're right. Our playgrounds were a little different, though."

Breaking the stare, I point to the red awning to our left. "True. We're heading right in there."

Logan leads the way, and once inside, we find ourselves seated at a booth with menus and a waitress heading away with our drink orders.

I promised myself there would be no liquor tonight so I wouldn't make any bad judgment calls like I did last night. Jesus. Logan probably thinks I'm some kind of split-personality psycho. I have to explain. Just like I do everything else, I barrel right into it.

"I was drunk last night. I told my friend not to let me drunk text, but I did it anyway."

Logan leans back in his chair, his gaze dropping to his menu for a moment. "I figured that much out myself."

"So we can forget that entire conversation ever happened?" My tone is hopeful, and probably a little naive for me. I grip the edges of the table while I wait for him to respond.

"Some of those things were pretty unforgettable, but I didn't drive twelve hours for that, Banner." His gaze is serious and intense, and I can't help but wonder if that's his normal state. "I'm not trying to be a dick when I say this, but I don't need to come all the way to New York just to get a piece of ass."

46

Something about his words has me relaxing my grip, and any momentary self-consciousness drains away.

"Look, you're hot. You know it. I know it. Unless the women in Kentucky are blind and stupid, I can't imagine it would be hard for you to get laid. Unless . . ." I pause and consider. "Do all Kentucky guys look like you? If so . . . holy crap."

He throws his head back, and his rich laugh resonates in the bar and causes a weird flutter in my chest.

Note to self: Don't let him laugh again. My body can't handle it.

When Logan finally stops, he drops his menu on the table. "Let me put it this way. If you've got all your teeth, don't live with your parents, and have a full-time job, you're pretty much a catch in Gold Haven."

My eyes widen at his words. "Then you're like the Holy Grail in BFE."

I realize my mistake as soon as he opens his mouth to laugh again.

"I don't know about all that, but if I were trying to catch a woman there, it wouldn't be too hard."

Apparently it wouldn't be too hard in New York either, because when a new waitress stops at our table to take our orders, she has to ask Logan to repeat his twice. It's not his accent that's giving her trouble . . . she's too busy memorizing every muscle of his body to pay attention to the words coming out of his mouth. She's not even attempting to be subtle, and it pisses me off.

Not because I'm jealous or anything. I swear.

"He said a cheeseburger. Medium rare. American cheese. Fries. Got it?" I repeat it for her a third time to confirm.

For the first time since she stopped at our table, she finally looks at me. Her perfectly arched eyebrows and perky tits might intimidate another woman, but not me. I stare her down and send the message that I will cut her if she doesn't move along.

She gets me loud and clear.

"Got it. Thanks." She flashes a quick look at Logan before backing away. "You let me know if y'all need anything else."

All of a sudden she's affecting a Southern drawl with that Jersey accent? Yeah . . . that's classy.

"Are the waitresses here all so damn forgetful?" Logan asks as she heads to a computer to put our order in.

"Only the ones who are dumb enough to wonder if you could be persuaded to take her home instead of leaving with me."

Logan's eyebrows shoot up and his features take on an insulted expression. "Are you serious? What the hell kind of guy does she take me for?"

"A shallow one, probably like all the others she's dated, and at least half the guys in this city."

My *real man* questions must be coming back to him, because he's quiet for a moment before he speaks again. "You really don't have a friggin' clue what a good guy is like, do you?"

I shrug. "They're not exactly in overabundant supply around here. They don't have to be. Maybe New York isn't all that much different from Kentucky, because if you've got the right job, the right clothes, and the right attitude, you can impress a lot of women."

Before he can reply, the waitress returns to the table with an obnoxious giggle. "I hate to bother y'all again, but I can't read my own writing. What did you want for your side, ma'am?"

You've got to be kidding me. The *ma'am* is a swipe at my age, and I know it.

"I ordered the same thing he did."

Embarrassment colors her cheekbones when she realizes her mistake. "Oh. Oops. I'll just go put that in for you."

"Thanks. We're both starving," Logan adds.

"I'll ask the kitchen to put a rush on it," she offers quickly.

Logan dismisses her with a nod before turning his attention back to me and reaching for his drink. "So, you gonna tell me how you got the name Banner? It's unique, for sure."

I smile and tell him the truth. "I'm named after the Hulk."

Logan is in the middle of sipping his beer, and nearly chokes. "The Hulk? As in the Incredible Hulk?"

I nod. "The one and only."

"Wait. Bruce Banner?"

"Yep. My parents are both über geeks, and my dad, despite being a world-renowned scientist, still has a comic book collection he won't let anyone touch. When they found out they were pregnant, my mom was positive it was some kind of mistake, so she wouldn't even discuss names. My dad picked Banner in honor of his favorite comic book scientist, and my mom didn't argue."

"You're lucky you didn't end up named Xavier," he says, in reference to Professor X of the X-Men.

"Or Logan," I say. "It suits you much better. You do have a sort of Hugh Jackman-esque look to you. Do you wear flannel shirts often? Or have metal claw thingies that shoot from your hands?"

"Adamantium claws, you mean?"

Shock slides through me as he throws out the correct term for the metal that makes up Wolverine's skeleton, one of those random Marvel facts from my childhood I've never forgotten.

"Oh my God, don't tell me you're a comic book geek too? I came by it genetically, so what's your excuse?"

Logan laughs and takes another sip of his beer, and I can't help but study his knuckles. No claws in sight, just big hands. They're a little banged up, which is probably normal for someone who works on cars all day, but they also look capable. There's no doubt in my mind, even after only spending a half hour with him, he's more *real man* than any guy I've ever met.

"I used to do odd jobs for the guy who owned the garage before me. Every Sunday, if I went to church, he'd make sure he had a comic book waiting for me after. It was something I looked forward to, and I think it was his way of doing a good deed, making sure I actually went."

"That was really cool of him. You said you finally bought the garage over a year ago?"

Logan nods. "Yeah, I came back from the Marines and needed a job, so he gave me back the one I had before I left. For some reason, when you join up, you think that your life is going to be different. And it is, while you're in the corps. But once you're out, sometimes it's like nothing but you changed. The entire world has gone on exactly the same way it did before, and there's no special prize for the fact that you put your life on the line for years. Sure, people appreciate your service, but that's where it ends."

"I never thought about it like that. How hard it must be to come back and not have anyone understand what you went through. To them, it's almost like you disappeared and then reappeared with no thought to what happened."

Logan shrugs. "It's a shame in a lot of ways, but then again, I'm one of the lucky ones. I made it back with all my limbs and my wits intact, and now I've got a thriving business of my own."

His pride when he mentions his business is plain, and I can't help but blurt out my own excitement.

"I'm hoping I'll be self-employed by this time next year too. I'm impressed that you've managed to come so far so fast. I hope I have half the success you do."

Logan leans forward in his seat. "You didn't mention that before."

The waitress chooses that exact moment to deliver cheeseburgers the size of my head.

"Is there anything else I can get you?" Her question is directed at Logan.

He looks to me. "Is there anything else you need, Banner?"

I glance at the condiments in the center and note that we've got all the ones I like. "Nope, I'm good. Thank you."

The waitress leaves, but Logan doesn't dive into his burger right away. "Tell me what you've got going on. I'm curious."

Part of me wishes I hadn't said anything, so I decide to keep it in vague terms. "I designed a couple of products and had some prototypes manufactured. Now I'm just finishing up the testing phase and gearing up for production soon."

"You going to tell me exactly what kind of products you designed?" Logan reaches for the condiments, and squeezes ketchup and mustard onto his burger.

I bite my lip, and for the first time since we sat down, I'm thankful when the waitress barges in again.

"Can I get you another round of drinks? The happy hour special on your beer is almost over, and I wouldn't want you to miss out."

Logan defers to me again. "You want another?"

"Sure. And a glass of water, as well."

As the waitress turns away, I take a giant bite of my burger, effectively ending the conversation.

TEN

Logan

MEETING BANNER IN PERSON HASN'T SATISFIED MY fascination with her. If anything, it's kicked it into high gear. It's easy to choose what impression you give someone via text messages, which is why I wanted to meet her face-to-face. I didn't think we'd have a damn thing in common, but that's not the case. After we stuffed ourselves with burgers and fries, she continues to politely dodge my question about what exactly her business is, and I let her.

I've never been the kind of guy to think a woman shouldn't be able to have any secrets. Besides, I'm still trying to figure out where this night might take us, because I already know I want to see her again.

I still haven't made sense of how the dirty text messages I got fit into the picture that's Banner Regent, but I hope once we get farther down this road, I'm going to find out.

She's different from any woman I've ever met. Confident. Self-assured. Not afraid to go after what she wants, and unapologetic about being herself.

Sexy doesn't even begin to cover her attitude.

And then when you add on the fact that she's got a killer body hiding beneath that green shirt-dress thing she's wearing, hair that a man can't help but want to see spread over his pillow, and whiskey-colored eyes that spark with a hint of mischief, you've got one hell of a package.

Smart, sexy, and a wildcat. But she lives seven hundred miles away, and it's not like I've got the kind of lifestyle where I can jet up to see her, or make that bitch of a drive again soon.

So, where does that leave us? I have no fucking clue, but I'm going to make the most of tonight, and see where she goes if I let her lead.

Instead of buying tokens, I throw down some cash to power up a swipe card so we can play some games.

When Banner heads right to the Skee-Ball, I can't help but laugh.

"What? I've seen this on movies and I've never played it. I have to try it."

"Shit, you've never played Skee-Ball?" I don't know why it surprises me, given what she's told me about her childhood with drivers, and parents who were too busy to spend time with her.

"Nope. Never. So you're going to have to school me in how this works."

There are a hell of a lot of things I want to school this woman in, but I'm sensing she might already be proficient in most of them.

I swipe my card on the machine, and the balls come down the shoot. "The goal is to get the balls into the holes and score the most points."

Banner leans over to pick one up, and even though I try not to stare at her ass, it's impossible to ignore how incredible it is.

"Balls in holes. I swear, all these games were invented by men."

I chuckle at her comment. "I'm sure you're right about that."

She pitches the ball overhand toward the hole, and when it hits the backboard with a *thwack*, Banner jumps. It falls to the bottom of the machine without scoring any points.

"I did that wrong, didn't I?" She tilts her head and stares at the game.

"You can make your own rules, but the traditional method is to pretend it's like a ski jump, I think." I pick up another ball and toss it underhanded so it slides up the ramp and flies into the center hole. "Like that."

A determined look crosses her face as she reaches for another ball. "I got this."

She sets out to prove she certainly does. Ball after ball, Banner lands them in the holes to rack up points, and each time, her excitement is obvious as she bounces and throws her hands in the air.

Her excitement is infectious, and I wrap my hands around her hips and pick her up as she scores the big points.

As soon as I touch her, my dick twitches against my jeans. *Fuck, she's sexy as hell.*

When I set her down, she presses a hand against each of my shoulders, grinning like crazy.

"This is so much fun. Why haven't I done this before?"

The excitement rolling off her hits me right in the gut.

"No idea, Bruce. No idea."

A smile tugs at the edges of her full lips. "Bruce, is it?"

"You can't tell me you hate it, because I won't believe you."

She tries to force the smile away, but is only partially successful. "Why's that?"

I lift a hand and skim my thumb over the dimple on her cheek. "Because this dimple pops out even when you're trying not to smile. It's a dead giveaway."

She bites down on her lower lip, and fuck, I've never wanted to kiss a woman more than I want to kiss Banner right now.

She leans in, and the subtle scent of citrus and something fresh drifts toward me, and my head instinctively lowers so I can take her mouth and find out if she tastes as good as she smells.

Her whiskey gaze connects with mine, and we both freeze. I see the desire there, but she's fighting it harder than I am.

Instead of moving in and taking what I want, I pull back. What happens or doesn't happen between us tonight is gonna be because she wants it every bit as bad as I do. That's the only way I work. I didn't drive up here for a booty call, and there's no way in hell I'm going to push her.

That said, if she gives me the sign, I'll have her up against the nearest wall so damn fast, she won't have time to second-guess the decision.

I step around her and reach down to grab another ball, then toss it so it lands in the center, racking up a few more points.

One ball remains in the chute.

"Last throw. All you."

Banner's smile faltered when I stepped away, but she rebounds quickly.

"The pressure . . . I'm not sure I can handle it." She reaches down to pick up the ball and tosses it between both hands. "Just kidding. I got this." She flashes a wink at me.

She releases the ball, and it hits the top right corner. She throws her arms into the air again. "I did it! I finally got the good hole!" She spins in a circle and catches a heel on the carpet, tumbling toward me.

This time, my arms close around her and her entire body presses against mine.

Fuck, she feels good in my arms.

"Careful there, killer. We've got a lot more games to play tonight."

The smile that flits over her face is pure temptation. "Yeah. We really do."

ELEVEN

Banner

I'VE NEVER WANTED TO JUMP A GUY'S BONES SO BADLY in my entire life. Ever.

Logan is like no other man I've ever met before. He's nice, but not in the way that makes him boring like the actuary I went out with once. He has this confidence about him that's unbelievably hot, and I like it way more than I should. How am I supposed to resist him when he says and does all the right things, and I can tell he's not putting on a show? Logan's just being himself, and somehow that's the sexiest thing I've ever encountered in my life.

And I want to ride him like a rodeo cowgirl on the back of a bull.

It only gets worse when I beat him at foosball—fair and square, I might add—and when I kinda-sorta throw myself into his arms, the sizable bulge in his jeans presses against me.

Holy Jesus.

This was supposed to be easy. Logan and I were supposed to meet, and I would send him on his way back to

Kentucky without falling into my old habits and sleeping with him.

But I'm terrified I'm losing the battle.

Right now, my hand is wrist deep in a bucket of cheese popcorn, and I'm staring at the most perfect ass I've ever seen encased in denim as he shoots basket after basket in hoops.

I stuff a handful in my mouth, reminding myself to chew as I'm riveted to the way his muscles move beneath his shirt. I'm not the only one, either. At least four other women are not-so-subtly checking him out, and I give them my best side-eye.

I've never been this territorial over a man before. It's new ground for me, and I'm not quite sure I know what to think about it. Logan turns around, and I miss my mouth and drop a few orange kernels to the floor.

How am I ever going to keep my hands off him?

I can't.

"We've got a few more credits on the card, so you get to pick next game. Then we can decide if we want to get more or just grab another drink."

I nod as I reach for another handful of cheese popcorn, but I have no idea how to respond.

Logan closes the few feet of distance between us and nods down at the bucket. "Am I going to lose a hand if I try to get some of that?"

His comment jerks me out of my momentary brain fade. "Sorry. No. Go ahead."

I shove the bucket into his hands and spin around, searching the lights and sounds for another likely game or machine. My attention lands on one I recognize from watching game shows with my parents' housekeeper. *Plinko*.

"That one." I point at the video game, which won't be quite as awesome as dropping the Plinko chips in myself, but I'm still pretty freaking excited.

"Why am I surprised you've seen the *Price is Right*?"

"Of course I have. I am American, after all."

He hands me the swipe card and holds out his arm. "All right. Lead the way."

I can feel him behind me every step, and I force myself to focus on the game ahead of me, and not the six-foot-something man behind me who I want to strip naked and drop to my knees in front of.

Not doing that. Not doing that. Not happening.

"You killed it at hoops. Did you ever play?" I ask in an effort to distract myself.

"Only in the desert while I was deployed. It was hotter than fuck, but we did the best we could to give the court some shade. I always liked football better, but when you're in the Sandbox, you take whatever distraction you can find."

It's hard for me to comprehend what it must have been like to go to war. I have so many questions, but I'm hesitant to delve into the subject further.

"You sound like you didn't hate it."

Logan swipes the card on the game, and I start to press buttons.

"I didn't. I liked being part of something bigger than myself. I liked the brotherhood. Outside of that world, you don't often meet people who would throw themselves on a grenade to save your life at the expense of their own."

"I can't even begin to imagine."

The look he gives me is once again serious and intense. "You shouldn't have to. Protecting people from having to experience the things I did is a big reason I stayed in the corps as long as I did."

Warmth floods me, and this time it's not between my legs.

"You're a good man, Logan Brantley. A really good man."

He shrugs, which I'm starting to recognize as a typical Logan response.

"I don't know about that, but I like to think I'm not a bad one." He nods at the game. "Let's have some fun."

I select the slot on the screen and release the Plinko chip. It lands on some kind of bonus slot, and the lights and sounds of the machine go wild.

"Looks like you just won yourself a jackpot."

I look Logan Brantley in the eye. "I could've told you that before we even started playing the game."

TWELVE

Banner

IT'S ALL HIS FAULT. THAT'S THE DEFENSE I'M GOING with as my limited willpower slips away a little at a time.

I told myself I wouldn't do this. But it turns out I'm a liar.

It's all his fault.

We walk up to the prize counter to cash out our tickets, and when we have the final tally, we both lean over the edge of the glass case full of prizes.

"You trust me to pick?" Logan asks.

"Go for it."

I'm actually excited to see what he chooses, and besides, now I can study him some more without him noticing. I've been doing it way too much tonight, and the more time I spend staring at him, the more I realize just how screwed I am.

He's not New York handsome in that slick, sophisticated kind of way. No, he's striking in a *holy shit, I don't even know if I can handle that intensity focused on me while I'm naked* kind of way.

Every time I speak, his attention is on me. He listens. Not just to figure out how he's going to reply, but in a way that seems like he truly wants to hear what I have to say. I don't think I've ever experienced it before, because I had no idea how sexy it is.

And that's on top of the rippling muscles under his shirt, the devastating grin, the scruff on his jaw, and the piercing blue eyes.

But I'm not truly aware of how screwed I am until he turns around, looking pretty damn pleased with himself.

"Close your eyes and hold out your hand."

My first thought is maybe he'll put his dick in it, but I shove that thought right out of my head because obviously we're in a public place. Maybe we could try this again later . . . *Stop it, Banner.*

"Why?"

"I picked something out for you."

I close my eyes and hold my palm up flat, and Logan drops something into it.

When I flick my eyes open, I look down and see a small Wolverine X-Men key chain in my hand. I lift my gaze to his, and he's holding a Hulk key chain dangling from his finger.

"Figured you could keep this to remember tonight. I don't think I'll be forgetting, but I like the idea of carrying a little Bruce home with me."

It's a key chain, I tell myself. It's not like he dropped a four-carat pink diamond in my hand. *But why does this feel more important in this moment?*

"Thank you. I'll keep it as a reminder." My words are

bullshit, because there's no way I'll ever forget tonight either. And what's more, I don't want it to end.

We turn away from the prize counter and walk toward the door. He helps me slip my trench coat on, and I belt it shut.

I can't let Logan get in that truck and drive back to Kentucky tonight. I can't.

He follows me outside silently, with his hand on the small of my back again. My heart, which was already hammering at an unhealthy pace, kicks up a couple of notches.

What am I doing? I honestly have no idea. If I take him home, I know I'm going to end up naked with him inside me. And then he'll be one more one-night stand for the books, because that's all I'm good at.

But what are my alternatives?

The silence hangs between us, and I have to say something as we make our way along the crowded sidewalk, the lights of Times Square surrounding us.

I make a snap decision. "You're not planning on driving back tonight, are you?"

"I figured I'd get out of the city and find a place to park, and sleep in my truck for a while before I drive the rest of the way home."

"I have plenty of room at my place. If your truck is parked in an overnight lot, you're more than welcome to stay."

He considers my offer for a few moments. "I'd appreciate that. And just so you know, I'm not expecting—"

I cut him off with a raised hand. "I know. Let's grab a cab."

I manage to flag one down, and give my address to the

cabbie as we slide into the backseat.

Logan's thigh presses against mine as the driver whips around a corner when he finds an opening in traffic, sending us both sliding across the seat.

"I got you," Logan says, wrapping an arm low around my hips to steady me.

He doesn't have me, though. Not really. But I want him to.

The cab stops in front of my building, and Logan pays this time before we climb out.

The doorman opens the glass door to the lobby when he sees me coming. "Good evening, Ms. Regent."

"Thank you, Joe. I appreciate it."

Joe says nothing about the man behind me.

Logan doesn't speak until we're inside the elevator. "Regent suits you. It's a hell of a name, but you carry yourself to fit it. You could definitely be the queen of something."

It's not one of those throwaway compliments like *you're beautiful* or *I love your eyes*. It's sincere, and more of my willpower evaporates.

"Thank you."

The ride up to my floor is borderline awkward as other building residents crowd inside with us, breaking the unwritten rule that you don't look at each other in the elevator. A middle-aged couple looks from me to Logan and back to me again, and I can see the judgment on their faces.

Another one-night stand, I'm sure they're thinking. It's not like I've ever tried to hide it. Why should I?

Regardless, I unlock the door to my apartment quickly. I don't want to tempt fate. The last thing I need is for Myrna to peek out with her cane in hand and hassle me, telling me to keep my legs shut.

Logan doesn't say anything about how fast I shut the door and lock it behind us. Instead, he takes in my apartment. It's done in whites and silvers and grays, with pops of yellow and turquoise. Nothing like what he would pick, I'm assuming, but I love it.

"Nice digs."

"I like it."

He turns to face me. "I like you, Banner. A lot. I didn't exactly expect tonight to go this well."

I press my lips together, unsure how to respond to his honesty, but I end up responding in kind. "Me either."

He lifts a hand to push a lock of hair away from my face. "A good surprise for both of us then, even though you're so fucking far out of my league, I should be back in my truck heading for the highway."

My mouth drops open. "I'm out of *your* league? Have you not seen yourself? Do they not have mirrors in Kentucky?"

"I'm nothing special. I make my living with my hands." He holds up both of them, big and wide, in front of me. "I spend more time scrubbing with Fast Orange so they're not stained black than you probably do getting your nails done. There's not one fucking thing about me that makes me the right guy for you. I've known that from day one."

His words cut into me, and I'm terrified he's going to leave me standing here without ever knowing what could have happened between us. If he's dead set on going, I'm not the kind of woman who will ever beg a man to stay.

"Then why did you come?"

Logan's gaze pierces mine. "I couldn't miss the chance

to meet a woman who has me intrigued like no one else ever has."

"Intrigued." I try the word out like it's Russian or something. *But isn't that exactly how I felt?*

"Yeah, really fucking intrigued."

"Well, you've met me."

Heat burns in his blue eyes. "And intrigued doesn't even begin to cover what I'm thinking right now. You're the whole package."

Even though I know I shouldn't, I peel off my trench coat and toss it toward the love seat. Without stopping, I reach for the belt on my dress and untie it.

If I thought I saw heat in his gaze before, now I see flames.

Logan steps forward and stills my hands when I go for the buttons. "I didn't come here to fuck you, Banner."

All my good intentions die a quick death.

"But I'm not letting you leave without fucking me either."

His hands tense on mine. "Then I'm gonna have to make it unforgettable."

My inner muscles clench at his drawled promise.

"This wasn't my plan," I tell him.

"Mine either, but now that you've started on those buttons, I want you to take it slow. I want to watch you unwrap every inch of that amazing body like the sweetest gift I've ever gotten."

He releases his hold on my hands, but I want his touch back. Somewhere else. Anywhere else.

One night. If that's all I'm going to get with Logan Brantley, then I'm going to make sure it stays with both of us for a lot longer.

Button by button, I undo my dress, letting the sides fall further open as each is freed. My plain black lingerie isn't anything that's going to bring a man to his knees, but Logan hasn't even looked down at what I'm revealing. His gaze is locked on my face, like he's waiting for something, and I'm strangely appreciative of it. It's not until I've unhooked every single button that he finally sweeps his gaze downward.

His groan is the most gratifying sound I've ever heard.

"Sweet Jesus, you've got a body made for sin."

I let the dress fall to my feet as his big hand slides into my hair to wrap around the base of my neck.

"How much do you trust me, Banner?" His words are quiet and low, sending goose bumps rising across my skin.

"What do you mean?"

"I'm the kind of man who likes what he likes and doesn't have a problem taking the reins. You strike me as a woman who might have a problem with that."

Heat flares between my legs.

"I don't like being told what to do unless I'm naked," I whisper. I'm pretty sure I have a T-shirt that says it too.

"Then I'm going to give us both what we want." His grip on my neck tightens, and I squeeze my thighs together in anticipation.

Tonight just might kill me. But it'll be worth it.

"Give me everything."

His eyes flash again, just before he lowers his lips to mine. My hands find their way to his shoulders, where I hold on as the kiss weakens my knees.

A strong arm slides under my ass to lift me higher and press me against his body. There's no give when solid muscle meets my curves, and I adjust my grip for a better hold. My legs snake around either side of his hips like I'm going to climb him—which isn't far off my plans.

The kiss goes on for long minutes as his tongue sweeps inside my mouth. I lose myself in it until he finally pulls back, giving him an inch to drag his lips down my jaw. Logan lifts me higher to tongue my nipple through my bra and tug at it with his teeth.

Shafts of pleasure dive from my nipples straight to my clit as it pulses against his hard stomach. I arch toward him, seeking more pressure as he unleashes waves of pleasure with his teeth and lips and tongue on my nipples.

When he slows for a moment, I breathe out what I believe passes for words. "Don't stop. Please. I'm so close."

He shoves my bra up, baring me, and continues tugging my nipple between his teeth. I writhe harder against his belly, grinding down until a totally unexpected orgasm bursts inside me. My eyes slam shut as I let it roll through me.

Holy shit, did that just happen?

THIRTEEN

Logan

I WAS HONEST WHEN I TOLD BANNER I DIDN'T COME here to fuck her, but that doesn't mean I haven't thought about it a hell of a lot, especially after her dirty drunk texts.

She could have had us stay at that tapas place and told me to have a safe drive home after dinner, and I wouldn't have held it against her.

But she didn't.

She also could have sent me on my way after having an amazing night at the arcade, and left it at that. I would have driven home to Kentucky with my brain working overtime on what kind of reason I could come up with to get my ass back to New York to see her again.

But she didn't.

When we walked into her apartment, I didn't have any plans except to let her set the pace. I wasn't about to step in and take over until she made it clear that's what she wanted. I can let a woman call the shots in a lot of areas of my life, but when it comes to sex, I like to be in control.

When she said she doesn't like to be told what to do unless she's naked, I knew Banner and I fit together better than I could have expected. When she comes from no more than my mouth on her tits and her pussy rubbing against my stomach, I don't need any more confirmation than that.

My cock is rock hard and ready to get in the game.

For a moment, I consider lowering her to the floor, but I don't want to let her out of my arms. Instead, I lift her higher, settling her middle over my shoulder as I cover her ass cheek with a hand to hold her steady.

I walk in what I assume is the direction of her bedroom and spot a king-sized bed covered in pillows and a fluffy blanket. First order of business: get on my knees and worship that sweet little pussy until she's come so many times, she forgets how insane this thing is between us. If I have anything to say about it, she won't have a chance to forget tonight, because this won't be the end.

Banner releases a breath when I lower her to the bed and tug off her sexy knee-high boots and the stockings beneath them.

"What—what are you—"

"You just got yourself off."

It's not a question, but she nods.

"And I want to get you off again. And again. I want to know how sweet you taste when you come against my mouth."

Her eyes widen as I rub the back of my fingers down the front of her panties. I'm glad they don't look like they cost hundreds of dollars, because I'm not promising I won't shred them to get them off her faster.

Pushing her legs apart, I settle my shoulders between

them and skim my thumb along the soaked fabric covering her slit.

"You're so fucking wet. I can't believe you came with just your nipples in my mouth. You're gonna come harder this time. And then even harder when I've got my cock buried inside you. Understand?"

She nods again.

"Good. Glad we're on the same page."

I pause and look up at her. The hunger builds in her whiskey-colored eyes, and my cock responds. I tug her panties to the side and see nothing but smooth skin.

"Did you wax this sweet cunt for me?" When Banner's eyebrows lift, I add, "Or does your pussy always look this perfect?"

I drag a finger along the edge, and she shivers against my touch. I know she wants more, but I want an answer first.

"You want me to make you come?" I ask.

Banner seems to have forgotten how to speak, because she nods for a third time.

"Then tell me."

She bites down on her sexy lip before opening her mouth. "I waxed just in case." Her answer comes out on a rush of breath.

"I like your *just in case* plan."

I lower my lips and devour her—sucking, licking, teasing, and finally sliding a finger inside to pump in and out before finding her G-spot and making her scream. Banner holds nothing back as she bucks against my face and cries out with her orgasm. Her uninhibited responses have me completely addicted.

There's very little that's more satisfying than knowing you can make a woman come like that. I wanted to be sure she'll remember me, but she's making it so I'll never forget her.

As I slide out from between her legs, someone pounds on the door with what sounds like a giant stick.

"What the hell?"

Banner slaps a hand over her eyes, and I swear I hear her count to ten under her breath.

The pounding continues.

"Pretend this didn't happen. Especially if I have to hide her body." She pushes off the bed and grabs her dress to slip it back on, doing up the buttons as she walks toward the door.

Given that comment, I get off my knees and pause at the bedroom doorway.

Banner opens the door. I can't see who's on the other side, but I stay put rather than moving to get a glimpse.

"The way you're carrying on is disgraceful. Everyone in the building can probably hear you, you hussy."

The voice carries into the apartment, and it sounds like Old Mrs. Rochester who lives down by the Four Corners in Gold Haven and routinely yells at children to get off her lawn.

"Can we not do this now? Or just pretend we're already done so I can get back to the best orgasms of my life, Mrs. Frances? I have some noise-canceling headphones you can borrow, because I can promise that's not going to be the last time I scream tonight."

"Disgraceful." The old woman huffs. "Apparently you didn't take heed of the advice I gave Sofia to pass on to you."

Banner leans against the doorway, and I catch a glimpse of fluffy white curls atop a very short old woman's head. I back up a step to make sure I stay out of sight. With the venom she's spewing, I'm sure my presence would only add fuel to the fire.

"If I'd kept my legs closed, I wouldn't have had that killer O, so I'm going to set your advice to the side and get off while I can. When I'm your age, I'll still have these memories. By the way, how'd you like the big black cock? Was it too much to handle?"

I choke down my laugh, wondering who the hell this old lady is for Banner to speak to her like that. It's clear this isn't a new style of conversation for them from their exchange.

"It's in the incinerator, where it belongs. You're never going to get any man to marry you if you insist on being such a tramp, you know."

Banner tilts her head to the side. "And since that's my only goal in life, I'll go cry into my pillow." Her voice drips sarcasm, but the tone changes dramatically when she continues. "Now, if you'll excuse me, Frau Frances, I have some very trampy activities to get back to. And I was serious about the noise-canceling headphones, because I'm pretty sure this guy will be able to go all night long."

The old woman hisses something else, but Banner steps back and shuts the door. When she turns around, she's trying not to laugh.

"Neighbor?" I ask.

"Yes. Mrs. Myrna Frances. It's her way of showing she cares."

I survey the gorgeous bombshell of a woman as she

walks back toward me, her hips swaying just enough to have my dick pressing hard against my zipper.

"Sounds like you two have some history."

Banner nods. "But I really don't want to talk about my ancient neighbor right now. I'm much more interested in picking up where we left off."

"Then get your ass over here, woman. Let's see how many times we can get her to bang on the door because you can't keep yourself from screaming."

FOURTEEN

Banner

ANY LINGERING THOUGHTS OF MYRNA FRANCES ARE banished as I walk toward Logan. I pause two feet away and unfasten my buttons again, letting the dress fall open a few inches.

"All the way off."

"You've already seen what's under it."

"That doesn't mean I don't want to see it again, and right fucking now."

"So you don't think I should take my neighbor's advice and keep my legs closed?"

A spark lights in Logan's eyes. "Only if you want your pussy to be even tighter while I fuck you."

Hearing those dirty words come out of Logan's mouth is my undoing. There's nothing sexier than seeing this nice guy turn dominant in the bedroom. My whole body responds, and I drop the dress in a puddle of material on the floor.

I'm really glad I didn't chicken out on meeting him. Really. Glad.

The last time a guy had the balls to order me around in the bedroom, he didn't have the skills to back it up. I know Logan can deliver orgasms purely based on his oral abilities, and I'm hoping he's just as talented with that bulge he's packing.

I try to slip by him, but his hands lock around my waist and his deep voice rumbles in my ear.

"I want you bent over the bed so I can get my hands on that perfect ass."

A shiver works through me as he releases his hold. "Is that right?"

"Don't make me wait, Banner. Stretch your arms out, palms down. Don't move them."

Following orders doesn't come naturally to me on my best day in any other area of my life, but there's something about giving up control in the bedroom to a man I'm confident can deliver that does it for me.

"Okay."

I close the remaining three feet to the bed and stretch myself over it, glad I picked the extra-high version and not the platform my designer tried to talk me into. This height is exactly perfect. I press my palms against the duvet and wait for whatever's coming next. The stroke of Logan's palm across the globes of my ass sends my anticipation soaring.

"Sweet fucking Christ." It comes out quietly, like he's saying some kind of prayer.

A guy who worships my ass? I can handle that.

Two fingers slide between my legs to sweep over my pussy, and I can't help but moan and push back against him. The one finger he gave me before had primed me, but I want more.

"Soaked pussy and a perfect ass." His thumb circles my clit, sending all the nerve endings spinning out of control. "This is pure temptation. Jesus, Banner. You're so sweet laid out for me."

His words set off another rush of moisture between my legs. I push back against his touch, wanting more.

Logan's other hand joins the game and both skim along my skin, teasing me, but never quite touching where I think they will. I press back again, trying to force him to give me what I want, but both palms lift before I feel a rush of air and a *crack* against my right cheek.

I jerk, sucking in a breath.

He spanked me.

A thought about my half-jokingly assembled sexual bucket list pops in my head. *I can finally check that off!*

His hand strokes the skin it just heated and I lean into it, already addicted to his touch on my skin.

"I love seeing my handprint on your ass."

"I can't believe you did that," I say, my voice barely a whisper.

"But you liked it."

His big hand finally slips between my legs again to drag through the slickness dripping down my thighs.

"You're so wet for me."

"I guess it's those magic Kentucky hands." When he pulls back, I regret the loss immediately and don't hesitate to tell him. "No stopping. We're moving to the fucking portion of the entertainment."

Logan leans over my body, his skin brushing against mine. His deep, accented voice sends shivers through me when he speaks.

"Fuck you with my fingers until you scream again? Because that's what I'm going to do. You're not ready for my cock yet. I won't give you that until you're begging for it."

I turn my head and look him in the eye. "I never beg for cock."

His low chuckle hardens my nipples as I squeeze my legs together.

"I guess it'll be a new experience for you then."

He cups my hip with one hand before landing another strike on my opposite cheek.

"What was that for?"

He soothes the burn with his lips this time, and it's several moments before he replies to my question. "Because I can."

The answer almost causes a spontaneous orgasm.

His hand slips between my legs again and one finger pushes inside, slowly dragging in and out until I'm bucking backward against it. I need more. I need all of him.

Logan takes his sweet time, teasing my clit, then fucking me with two fingers, before I'm tumbling toward desperation.

One word falls from my lips. "Please."

He stills. "Please, what?"

"Please just fuck me already!" The demand is as ragged as my need.

Logan trails a finger down my spine, stopping just above my ass. "You did say *please*."

He steps back, and I hear the telltale sound of a zipper and the tearing of a package.

"You sure you can handle this?"

Shockingly, I haven't handled it. I haven't even gotten

a palm on Logan's cock because this foreplay has been all about me. I can't remember the last time that happened.

"Yes," I tell him, my reply to his question delayed, but honest. "I can handle whatever you give me."

The blunt head of Logan's cock slides between my legs and nudges against my opening. But he doesn't push inside. No, he slides further, and moans of pleasure escape my lips as the head of his cock teases my clit.

Logan Brantley is literally the biggest cock tease I've ever met.

"Please. Just . . . please." The words are out before I realize I'm begging again.

He has me breaking all my rules, and I can't find it in me to regret it right now.

He freezes. "I love how greedy you are for my cock. Greedy and needy. It's the perfect fucking combination."

He slows his sensual torture by once again notching the head of his cock against my entrance. "Not that I had any doubt you'd be fucking perfect, Banner." With a single thrust, he buries himself inside me.

I suck in a breath at the shock to my system. Thick and long, his cock fills every inch of me before he pauses and groans.

"So goddamned tight."

Logan begins to move, pulling back and rocking inside, his hand sliding around my hip to cover my clit and force me to the edge. My arms wobble, and I drop to my elbows as he fucks into me with deep, measured strokes.

I open my mouth to scream, but bury my face in the duvet to muffle the sound. If anyone were to interrupt us, I might commit murder.

My orgasm tears through me, and with the constant pressure on my clit, the waves of pleasure don't stop. I lose track of time as Logan continues to fuck me into oblivion. My elbows give out and I collapse onto my forearms. When he pulls out, I open my mouth to protest, but before I can form words, he flips me onto my back.

"I'm not done with you. Not even close."

He lifts me up and slides me down his hard body. My hands wrap around his cock and guide it inside me again.

Fuck. Me.

With both hands gripping my ass, Logan lifts and lowers me, powering inside with each stroke.

The pressure on my clit unleashes wave after wave of pleasure. My nails dig into his shoulders as I scream out with another shattering orgasm. Moments later, Logan throws his head back and roars out his own climax.

When he carefully lowers me back to the bed, I'm pretty sure I've been fucked to death. My eyelids flutter as he pulls out and steps away, but I don't move.

I never want to move again.

Warm heat glides between my legs, and I open my eyes. Logan's cleaning me up with a washcloth.

He's sweet too, I think, just before I pass out.

Someone knocking on the door wakes me up, but all I want to do is pull a pillow over my head and go back to sleep.

Heat radiates from the man beside me. Logan's dark head is turned away, and I'm thankful the pounding hasn't woken him. This is one morning after I have no idea how to handle.

Last night was amazing. Beyond amazing, if I'm being honest. And yet I have absolutely no idea what I'm supposed to do now. I screwed up. I totally screwed up.

I one-nighted the nicest, most genuine guy I've ever met and had amazing sex, and now it's over.

What is wrong with me?

The knocking comes again.

I don't need to listen to Mrs. Frances deliver a morning-after lecture either. But the upside? If she's outside my door, at least she survived the night, and I didn't cause a heart attack with my screaming.

My phone starts next, and that I'm definitely not ignoring. It's the *Golden Girls* theme song, and that ringtone only belongs to one person—my best friend, Greer.

I roll off the bed, grab my phone from the nightstand, and snag the first shirt I see before tiptoeing out of the room. I pull the door far enough closed not to make it squeak, and pull on Logan's white T-shirt before I answer.

"What's goin' on, G?"

I want to blurt out everything that has happened since I talked to her last, but I know what she's dealing with is so much more important. Besides, how do I tell her I just added Logan Brantley to the notches on my bedpost? *God, I suck.*

She's going to want answers about what's happening next, and I don't have any. Nope. All I have is a night of memories, and no freaking clue what to do now.

"Sorry. Did I wake you?"

"Um, yeah. No biggie. What's going on?" I say in a low voice, trying to keep my voice down so I don't wake Logan.

"I'm outside your door," Greer says, and my gaze darts

toward it.

"Oh. Shit. Okay. Hold on."

I race to the door, unhook the chain, and throw the dead bolts before opening it just enough to peek out.

She takes one look at me in what is clearly not my shirt, and her eyebrows go up. "Am I interrupting?"

Her tone is nonjudgmental, but that doesn't matter when I'm so busy beating myself up over what I did.

I shake my head but keep the door where it is. If I tell Greer who is in my apartment, she's going to want details, and I don't want to admit that I treated him exactly like every other guy, which is the opposite of what I promised myself I would do. As much as I can use my best friend's advice right now, this is something I have to deal with myself.

"No, of course not. You're never an interruption. What's up?"

From behind me, I can hear Logan say my name from the bedroom. His voice gets louder as he comes into the living room, and my grip on the door tightens. *Please don't come out here.*

I slide the door closed a fraction of an inch, strike a casual pose, and turn the conversation back to Greer. "What's happening? You're awfully dressed up for an unemployed Saturday morning. When did you get back? Did they give a cause of death? What's happening?"

My leg bounces of its own accord, mostly because I want to spring through this space between us and hug my friend and spill my guts like I normally would, but it's time for me to fix my own damn problems. At least I'm not dealing with funeral arrangements like she is.

I force my leg to still, but Greer is eyeing me like I'm

acting crazy. Luckily for me, crazy is actually my normal.

"Uh, yesterday. Not yet on the autopsy. I just wanted to see if you were up for grabbing lunch. But we can do it tomorrow or whenever."

I nod at her suggestion. Maybe tomorrow I'll have my shit figured out. *And tomorrow Logan will be gone, because I one-nighted the only guy who has ever liked me for* me. *Good job, Banner.*

The thought slams into me like a gut punch. I pull myself together enough to answer Greer.

"Tomorrow's good. I want all the details. Call me?"

I hear Logan again behind me and I panic, smiling and shutting the door on my best friend.

Now I have to face what I did. Well, the man I did, anyway.

It's official. I suck at life.

FIFTEEN

Logan

I WATCH AS BANNER CLOSES THE DOOR AND TURNS around to rest her back against it. "Was there a reason you didn't want Greer to know I was here?"

Her gaze jerks up to mine. "She doesn't need to know."

"Why's that?" I'm not sure why I ask, because part of me can already see the writing on the wall.

"I just . . . I didn't want her to think . . ."

Memories of hiding in a closet when I was seventeen while Tessi Lee's father stormed into her bedroom come rushing back and hit me hard. I didn't used to be the kind of guy a girl wanted to be with out in the open before, and it seems that even though over a dozen years have passed since that incident, Banner Regent sees me the same way as girls in Gold Haven did when I was a teenager going nowhere fast.

For some fucked-up reason, I want to hear her admit it. "Didn't want her to think what?"

Banner shrugs. "You've met Greer. She likes to work out everything in her head, and if she saw you here she'd have questions, and I don't have answers. She'd undoubtedly make this into a huge deal, and it doesn't need to be."

I know I'm kidding myself to think it's going to make a difference, but I tell her what I'm thinking anyway. "I don't know about you, but last night was a pretty big deal to me."

Her gaze drops to the floor. "But that doesn't mean anything changes today. We have totally different lives." As if she found the balls to tell me to my face, Banner finally meets my eyes. "We can still be friends, though, right?"

Her words hit me with more force than I anticipated. I turn on my heel and head for the bedroom. After grabbing my jeans, I yank them on and snag my wallet and phone off the nightstand. Banner watches from the doorway.

"Friends?" I say, my tone harsh. "Is this how you treat your friends? Why should I be surprised one night is all I'm good for?"

She crosses her arms over her chest—over my damn shirt. "That's not what I mean—"

"Then what do you mean, Banner? How 'bout you explain it to the dumb redneck slowly, in small words."

"What else can we possibly be but friends when I live here and you live in BFE?"

I cross my arms to match her posture. "I guess we'll never know."

"I'm sorry."

"Don't fucking apologize for deciding that you can't open your eyes for five seconds to realize that this wasn't just another hookup. But I guess that's why you didn't want Greer to know. Didn't want to explain that you fucked the redneck. What would she think of you then?"

Banner drops her hands, but they're balled into fists.

"You're twisting my words. I didn't mean—"

"I'm pretty sure you don't have a fucking clue what you mean. If you'll just give me my shirt, I'll get the hell out of your way. I got a long drive back to BFE."

She looks down at the T-shirt and back up at me. "Maybe—"

Honest to Christ, I don't want to hear any more. My pride has already taken enough of a beating. Fuck the shirt.

"Never mind. Keep it."

Her face falls. "I'm sorry, Logan. I didn't mean to—"

"Save it. I'm done here."

But she's already stripping it over her head and tossing it at me.

"Just take it."

Her voice shakes on the last word as I force myself to look away from her naked body. A dumb redneck like me should probably be happy I got to have her for one night. But the funny thing is, I wanted more, and now it just pisses me off.

"Have a nice life, Banner. Good luck with whatever the fuck you're doing."

With my shirt clutched in my hand, I stride to the door and don't look back.

SIXTEEN

Banner

K ARMA IS SUCH A BITCH.

This week is supposed to be an amazing one. I'm supposed to be approving the prototypes as they finish the testing phase, and gearing up to schedule my first production run.

But one of the models had a minor malfunction, so after some quick fixes, the factory was supposed to send a replacement. Instead, they sent two dozen. To my office. The boxes were stacked up all around my cube, and when my asshole cube neighbor decided to open one, chaos ensued.

Now I'm sitting at the curb on top of a stack of boxes, waiting for a car and driver I'm not going to be able to afford for much longer since I no longer have a job because of some stupid no-moonlighting policy.

If you ask me, it's a ridiculous policy. Basically, I'm not allowed to have any other kind of employment or business interest that's not approved in advance, in writing, by the company. Since I didn't read the employee handbook cover to cover, I wasn't aware. But I'd signed a statement saying I'd read it and agreed to everything inside.

My explanations and excuses didn't sway HR or my boss. In fact, they probably helped in the decision to terminate my employment immediately.

Because it bears repeating, I'll say it again. Karma is a bitch.

It's been exactly four days since Logan Brantley walked out of my apartment and left me feeling like shit on his shoe. I know it's my fault, and the guilt has been eating at me.

Maybe if I hadn't botched that so completely, I wouldn't have spent this entire week picturing every woman in that Podunk town coming into his garage to get some *work* done on their *chassis*.

It's probably what distracted me into using the autofill address option and picking my office as the ship-to location for the factory.

As rain pelts down on me, I try to find a bright side. I have a lot more time to devote to the work I actually want to do instead of the job that was grinding away at me.

I've dumped almost all my cash into my business, but I have enough left in the bank to float me for a short time while I figure out my finances and how I'm going to pay for my life until the first production run is out in the market. My trust fund only allows me to take out a certain amount each year, and I hit that limit for my start-up costs two months ago.

As my car pulls up, I feel a certain sense of relief. Maybe getting fired will be the best thing that ever happened to me. Or I'm going to get evicted, end up living in a cardboard box and eating out of Dumpsters. *No. Definitely not.*

I'm arranging for the doorman to bring the boxes inside when Frau Frances shuffles into the lobby with Jordana twirling on her leash, and Irene, another of her caretakers, by her side.

Of course, the first thing she spots is me with my file box of crap I cleaned out of my desk.

"Don't tell me you got fired."

Her voice carries through the entire lobby, and several heads swivel in my direction as Jude, the daytime doorman, pushes a hand truck full of the other boxes toward the service elevator to deliver to my apartment. Why didn't I give him this one too?

I try to brazen it out. "Why would you assume I got fired? I could have quit."

I'm honestly not in the mood to pick a fight with Myrna today, and am relieved when another resident joins us in the elevator. Maybe an audience will tone down her acerbic attitude.

"You're not dumb enough to quit when you know that the association bylaws and your lease require that to be a resident in this building, you have to be gainfully employed or able to prove that you have regular and substantial income coming in every month from other means, or have a substantial minimum bank balance."

Her words hit me like a subway train. "Excuse me?"

"Didn't you read your lease?"

Of course I didn't, but I can't tell her that. "That can't be legal."

"It is if you agreed to it in writing. I was on the association board when we instituted the change after the dot-com bubble. Too many residents were losing their jobs and life savings, and we didn't want them taking up space here while we waited to evict them through traditional means. If you'd purchased your apartment when you moved in, you wouldn't have an issue."

Jordana pops up on her back feet to paw at my thigh. I bend down to give her a pat, but my heart isn't in it.

This can't be right. *And why didn't I buy to begin with?* Oh, right, because I thought having a mortgage sounded like a bad idea.

"What does regular and substantial income from other means mean?" I ask her.

"That's for tenants who live on pensions and such. You have to prove you receive a deposit every month."

Which wouldn't be a problem if I'd budgeted for monthly deposits from my trust, but that's out of the question now, and my bank balance isn't going to impress anyone.

"Surely there's some kind of grace period for that. They're not just going to notify me tomorrow that I have to move out because I got fired."

The elevator stops on the eleventh floor, and the other female passenger gives both Mrs. Frances and me the side-eye before stepping off.

Surprisingly, Mrs. Frances doesn't come back at me with both barrels blazing. "I guess you better read the association bylaws and your lease then, because I don't recall the grace period. That association board has always been cutthroat, and apartments in this building are highly sought after. Do you know how many people are hoping I'll die so they can buy mine? It's basically the only reason I get out of bed every day and go do that horrible yoga stuff—so I can live forever and screw them all over."

I believe every word she says.

Meeting her faded blue eyes, I say, "Please, just . . . don't say anything to the association. I have a way to make a living. I just need a few months for it to all come together."

She narrows her gaze on me. "You're going to become a call girl, aren't you? Not that you shouldn't get paid for what you're giving away for free."

I choke on air. "Excuse me?"

"I'm just saying, if that's how you're going to make a living, I'm not keeping quiet for that."

The elevator slows on our floor, and I answer as the doors open. "No. No, I'm not becoming a call girl."

She harrumphs and trudges down the hall with her cane in hand. "I guess we'll see about that."

Before I can counter, Mrs. Frances is already halfway into her apartment with Irene shooting me sympathetic looks over her shoulder and Jordana yipping at the door.

I'm so screwed.

SEVENTEEN

Logan

I REACH INTO THE TOP OF MY TOOLBOX TO FIND A pencil, and when my hands touch satin, I mentally kick my own ass. There's seriously something wrong with a man who steals a pair of panties and keeps them in his toolbox. And probably a special place in hell for the fucker who stops to touch them in the middle of the workday.

Shoving them aside, I grab a pencil and write down the VIN of the car that I just agreed to restore. Something about it is rubbing me wrong, and not just the fact that I don't know how Lonnie Benson got the cash to buy a '69 Camaro. He's gotta be cooking meth in his trailer because I would have heard if he'd won the lottery.

My job isn't to speculate, and a basic restoration that promises to bring me at least five grand in profit isn't something I can turn down, so I took the job. But first, I'm going to run the VIN to make sure the car isn't stolen. That's the last thing I need to get tangled up with.

When the lead on my pencil breaks, I reach back into

the top of my toolbox and once again feel the fabric of the panties I've sworn every day I'll throw away. And yet here I am, alone after another twelve-hour day, and they're not in the bottom of my trash.

Why haven't I tossed them? A better question is why in the hell I took them to begin with. Something about Banner Regent fucked me up in a big way.

I've tried everything I can think of to stop thinking about her . . . except get rid of the reminder.

The front-door chime rings as I shove the panties under a pair of gloves. I should have locked the door after Lonnie left, but I was too busy checking out the car.

I turn to see Emmy Harris picking her way across the garage, carrying an honest-to-God picnic basket.

"I swear, you're going to have to leave work one of these days before dark."

Her curvy body is poured into tight jeans that are tucked into expensive tooled-leather cowboy boots. Not the kind of boots she'd wear to the restaurant either, because they look way too fancy. There's nothing about her outfit that says *I was just in the neighborhood.*

It's not hard to recognize a woman on the hunt in this town. Apparently Emmy's done waiting for me to come to her.

"Whatcha got there, Ms. Harris?"

She smiles. "Oh, nothing too exciting. Just some chicken and dumplings, and an apple pie. I was trying out a new recipe for the restaurant and thought you could give me your opinion. I know you've got a powerful taste for chicken and dumplings."

I think about the panties in the top of my toolbox, and

decide *why not.* It feels better to have a woman bringing you dinner than it does to have one hiding your existence from her best friend.

"That's awfully kind of you to think of me."

Her smile turns even sweeter. "You know I think about you all the time, Logan. How about we eat in the waiting room instead of in the middle of all this." She waves a hand, gesturing to the shop.

"I'll follow you."

And that's how I ended up eating dinner on paper plates in the waiting room of my shop with Emmy Harris, while all the people driving by the Four Corners could no doubt see us plain as day. *At least she wants to be seen with me, even if it is just to stake her claim.*

As we finish up the apple pie—which, she reminds me, is a county fair blue-ribbon winner—she sets her paper plate aside and crosses her legs.

"I wouldn't normally dare be this bold, but I have to ask . . . when are you finally going to ask me out on another date, Logan?"

I can't help but wonder if Julianne spilled about me texting another woman, and that's what's causing Emmy to be more forward than normal. Then again, Julianne and Emmy get along as well as cats and water.

I shove a bite in my mouth to buy myself some time to answer. *Why am I putting her off?* She's a nice woman, a great cook, and she doesn't give off the blatant looking-for-a-man-to-be-a-paycheck vibe.

It's not like the woman whose panties are in my toolbox is ever going to be a real possibility.

I'm throwing them away.

"How does this weekend sound?"

Emmy's smile flashes triumphantly, and I wonder if I've made a mistake.

EIGHTEEN

Banner

FOUR DAYS. THAT'S HOW LONG IT TAKES BEFORE THE notice from the association shows up in my mailbox.

I skim over the paper, wondering why Frau Frances would do it. I didn't think she hated me enough to rat me out and get me evicted. According to the notice, I have five business days to show either proof of gainful employment, some other means of steady income, or a fat bank balance—to be evaluated at the sole discretion of the association—or my lease will be null and void.

After the few crazy weeks Greer's had, including quitting her corporate lawyer job, the last thing I want to do is bother her with this mess. Then again, she already dragged all the Logan stuff out of me when I delivered the news about getting fired, so I've got nothing left to hide. It's not like I can afford another lawyer at this point, and then there's the fact that she'd kill me if I didn't ask her for help.

I snap a picture of the notice and text it to her, along with a note to check her e-mail in five minutes. I forward a copy of the lease to her, then sit down with my trusty bottle of vodka and wait.

My phone rings ten minutes later, and I snatch it up. "This can't be legal!"

"I really, really hate to tell you this, but you agreed to this ridiculous draconian rule when you signed your lease. Did you actually read these rules?"

I cringe, my tiny ray of hope dimming as my former legal eagle delivers the bad news.

"Nope. Sure didn't. Just like I didn't read the no-moon-lighting policy in the HR handbook that got me fired."

"I'm so sorry, B. Do you have another means of income you can show them? Monthly deposits into your account in an amount no less than four times your rent from any-where? How about your trust fund? Can you have the trust-ee do monthly payments?"

I lower my head to the counter and smack my forehead against it. "No, I can't. It's maxed out this year."

There's a moment of silence on the other end of the line before Greer replies. "Okay. Let's think."

I love that she doesn't question how I spent the money, even though I know she must be wondering. I haven't told her about my new venture because I didn't want to spill un-til I knew it wasn't going to be yet another big idea of mine that crashed and burned. Also, I know she'll offer to help any way she can, and this time, I feel like I have something to prove. Like I can succeed or fail based on my own merits. *Holy shit, I might be growing up.*

"Can you get your parents to float you?"

I actually laugh at her suggestion. "No way in hell. You know how they are."

Greer sighs. "Will you let me help? You know I have

the cash."

"I love you so freaking much, but there's no way I'm taking your money. Maybe . . . I'll go talk to my parents. Last-ditch effort for desperate times. Where the hell am I going to live if I lose this apartment and have no income?"

"If you'd just let me help—" Greer starts, but I cut her off.

"Let me try to figure this out myself first."

"Okay, but you can always crash at my place. You'd do it for me."

She's right, but I'm not taking a handout, at least not from anyone who isn't blood related. "It's time for me to learn how to handle my shit myself, I think. Don't worry; I'll figure it out."

"Damn right you will. You're Banner Fucking Regent."

I smile at my best friend's confidence, and hope I can prove I deserve it. "I'll woman up or get the hell out of the city, I guess."

Greer is quiet for another long moment. "Let me know if there's anything at all I can do. You know I'll do it."

"Talk soon, babe."

She says good-bye, and we hang up.

I stand in the middle of my apartment and turn in a slow circle. "They're only walls." I swallow back the rising lump in my throat. "I can figure this out."

It's not like I have a choice.

I head for my bedroom to change into the armor I'll need to face my parents.

God help me.

Jansen and Jane Regent live in a house they've owned for as long as I can remember. While I was growing up, we bounced between Manhattan and the three-acre estate that still boasts green shag carpet from the '70s and the ugliest avocado-green appliances you can imagine.

It's not like they don't have the money to renovate, but my parents would never take the time to deal with that kind of project when they can hole up in their state-of-the-art lab they built only twenty yards from the house. Actually, I'm pretty sure the lab and its contents are worth triple what the house and the land are.

What exactly do my über-genius parents do? Freelance research and development for biotech and defense contracting firms that's so top secret, they can't even talk about it to their daughter. Not that they would if they could.

My mother still hasn't forgiven me for the C I got in AP Chemistry in tenth grade (on purpose, I might add, so I could screw over my GPA and any chance of getting into MIT). I believe that day was when she officially gave up on me ever following in their footsteps. My mother doesn't blink at dropping a million dollars for super-special mice for their lab, but the chances of her offering to bail me out for a fraction of that amount are slim to none. And yet, given that I'm up shit creek with no paddle, I'm going to sacrifice my pride and give it a shot.

When I knock on the door to the house, Albright, my parents' jack of all trades, answers the door.

"Ms. Banner, it's a surprise to see you here."

I'm sure it is a surprise, because generally I only show up for one or two federal holidays, and usually leave as quickly as possible.

I give Albright a quick hug and step inside. "Are my parents available?"

He smiles. "They're in the lab. I can check with them to see if they're able to take a break to speak with you, though."

As much as I want to change my mind and tell him not to bother so I can turn around and walk away, I decide I can't waste the Uber fare I spent to get out here if there's a chance in hell they'll help.

"That would be great."

Albright disappears into the kitchen, no doubt to exit out the back and find my parents. He reappears five minutes later. "Do you want me to fix you something to eat? It will be about thirty or forty-five minutes before they can take a break."

I should have figured this wouldn't be a quick process.

"A drink would be fabulous."

Albright's smile becomes strained. "Your parents don't drink anymore, so this house is dry now."

Wow. That's a first.

I study the older man for a moment. "I bet the house isn't completely dry."

Albright has lived on the premises for the last ten years or so, and I raided his liquor collection once upon a time when he first moved in. He got smart pretty quick and locked it up. Why he didn't rat me out to my parents, I have no idea.

One corner of his mouth edges up. "I may be able to get you a Scotch."

"I would be forever indebted to you. This isn't a conversation I'm sure I can handle without liquor."

He nods and disappears in the direction of the butler's

quarters. When he returns, it's with a small tumbler of Scotch, neat. Three fingers, if I'm not mistaken.

Albright hands it to me with a sober expression. "This stays between us."

I accept the glass and grip it with both hands like it's the key to surviving this afternoon, which it might very well be.

"You know I'm not going to tell." I sip and hide my grimace. Scotch has never been my favorite. "Speaking of which, why didn't you ever tell my parents I stole your booze when I was seventeen? They probably would've shipped me off to boarding school immediately."

He doesn't answer right away. "Maybe because I didn't think you needed to give them another reason to find fault with you."

His words sting, but they're the truth.

"They never needed help finding reasons." I down the rest of the Scotch in three small sips. "But enough about my fondest childhood memories. How are you these days? Are you ever going to retire?"

"I'm quite acceptable. My health is good, and your parents are generally easy to please as long as I keep to their requirements. I'm not sure I'll ever retire at this point."

I want to ask about his children, because I'm pretty sure Albright has two sons he doesn't see often, but unless he brings it up, I'll leave the subject alone.

"Fair enough."

"And yourself, Ms. Banner? What brings you here today?"

I think about the complete and utter shit show my life has turned into seemingly overnight. Deciding to spill it all to Albright, I unload.

"I'm getting evicted because I lost my job, and if I can't prove that I have money in the bank or a steady income stream, I have to be out of my apartment in a week."

Albright's silvery-gray eyebrows climb upward as I drain my glass.

"Really? That's terrible. Shouldn't you be able to prove an income from your grandparents' trust?"

It's not surprising that Albright knows about the trust. "I've hit the max for withdrawals this year. I don't have anything else to show for it—yet. I just need some time."

He's silent for several long moments before speaking. "And you're here for your parents' assistance with this financial issue?"

I nod slowly. "I'm not expecting a great outcome, but it's either this or a cardboard box down on Skid Row somewhere, and I'm not asking my friends for help."

Albright reaches for my empty glass. "I'll get you another." He doesn't have to say anything else. It's clear that he knows my parents will say no.

So, why am I even bothering with what is sure to be an incredibly humiliating episode? Probably because my options are limited, and I'm hoping for some kind of miracle.

Unlikely.

I sip the next glass of Scotch more slowly, letting it mellow me out. When Albright takes the empty glass away, I know I only have a few more minutes before my parents will appear. The timing is almost perfect, because the back door opens and in they come.

They're not clad in lab coats and safety glasses like one might expect. My father is dressed in pressed khakis with a knife-like crease down the front and a white button-down shirt. My mother is wearing a black skirt, white blouse, black cardigan, nylons, and ugly shoes. They look like they're headed on a Sunday drive rather than stepping out of a state-of-the-art lab.

"This is certainly a surprising interruption," my mother says. Her use of *surprising interruption* rather than *pleasant surprise* doesn't bode well.

"Banner, how are you?" my father asks.

"Thank you for taking a few minutes out of your busy schedule to see your only daughter. I appreciate it."

An unavoidable edge of bitterness creeps into my tone, even though I try to keep it out. But at the end of the day, *I am bitter.* They spend more time worrying about the mice that live in the lab than they do about me.

"We only have fifteen minutes before the next set of results needs to be recorded, so you'll have to excuse us if this seems brief." My mother might as well be talking to a stranger, for all the friendliness in her voice.

"I'll make it quick then," I say, thankful for the warmth of the Scotch pooling in my belly. "I need to borrow some money."

My parents' eyes meet before either responds.

"Absolutely out of the question," my mother replies.

"You have your own money, as you so frequently like to remind us," my father adds.

"I just need to have it in my bank account. I won't even spend it. If I don't have it, I'm going to get evicted."

My father's salt-and-pepper brows draw together. "Evicted? For what reason?"

Deep breath, Banner. "I lost my job, and apparently there's a clause in my lease that says you have to be employed or have an income from other means to continue to lease an apartment."

"You lost another job?"

I would like to say my mother sounds surprised, but she really doesn't. My employment history isn't exactly studded with employee-of-the-month plaques, which is why I know my future is being my own boss.

But I can't tell my parents about the business I'm working on. Not only will they disapprove, they'll tear my ideas to shreds. Scientific method, my ass.

"Yes, I got fired. Again."

My mother sends my father a look that says *I have no idea where we went wrong, do you?* His silent response agrees that this is not their fault.

"Never mind," I say, holding up a hand. "I should have known better than to think my parents would care that their only child is going to be evicted from her apartment with minimal notice."

"You need to learn to manage your trust fund better. What kind of parents would we be if we didn't allow you to face the consequences of your own actions?"

I want more than anything to scream *the kind that care*, but there's no point in emotional displays when you're dealing with Jansen and Jane Regent.

Hello, homelessness. We're going to become well acquainted.

I straighten my spine and give both of them a nod. "I don't want to keep you. I'll let you know where I end up eventually."

"This kind of self-pity isn't constructive, Banner. I hope you learn something from this experience to apply to future situations," my mother says.

Life is just one big science experiment to them.

The disapproving look on my mother's face deepens her crow's-feet, and I have another concrete reason to strive to be her opposite. Wrinkles from being a judgmental cow require Botox, and I'm terrified of botulism.

"Thanks for the tip, Mom. I'll get right on that."

NINETEEN

Banner

I TOLD MYSELF I WOULDN'T LAY THIS ON HER DOORSTEP because it's not her problem, but my first call is to Greer.

She gets straight to the point when she answers. "What did your parents say?"

"About what you'd expect. They're not going to help. Such a shocker, and not in a good way like when a guy decides to surprise you with a finger in your ass."

Greer chokes out a laugh, but cuts it off just as quickly. "Crash at my place. It's fine."

I shake my head, even though she can't see it. "I can't. Don't freak out, but I actually put together a rough budget on the Uber ride to my folks', and I need to cut all my expenses to the bone if I want to buy myself some time. I think I have to leave Manhattan."

A few moments of silence stretches between us before she replies. "I know you told me it didn't end well, but . . . I have an idea."

"What are you talking about?"

"Logan."

"What?" Shock forces the word out at about twenty decibels louder.

"Jesus, no need to yell. Just hear me out. Do you want to see him again?"

I could kick myself for how fast the word *yes* pops out of my mouth.

"I think I might have a solution for you. I started thinking about it earlier, but I wasn't sure you'd go for it. Now, though, if you're thinking you need to leave the city anyway, it could be kind of perfect."

"What are you talking about?" I'm not following her.

"I'd have to talk to my brother first, but Holly still has her gran's house in Kentucky, and from what I could tell, it's a pretty inexpensive area. She doesn't need to be worrying about it with the baby, so if you don't have an issue seeing Logan again . . . I was thinking you could work out a deal to housesit for Holly to make sure the place stays in good shape."

The wheels start turning in my brain immediately.

Kentucky?

BFE?

Logan?

A cheap place to live. A break from the rat race.

A fresh start.

I can work from anywhere as long as I'm only going to be working for myself. All my communications are online, and as long as the factory can ship to me . . . this might actually work.

"Are you for real? You think they'd let me? I'd pay rent, though. I don't want anything for free."

Even if the rent is a quarter of what I'm paying in New York, I can swing it.

"Let me make a call and I'll get back to you. But if I know both of them, I'd say it's time to start packing your stuff."

"I have to do that anyway, so I might as well get on it."

"You want me to come help?"

I know Greer doesn't have time to spare with everything going on in her life right now, but she's the kind of friend who would drop it all to help me anyway.

"No, I can take care of all of this. Just let me know what they say."

"I'll call you back as soon as I know something."

"Love you, Greer."

"Love you, B."

When I hang up the phone, I focus on not getting my hopes up. There could be a million reasons why this won't work. I lift my feet onto the couch and wrap my arms around my knees to hug them close to my chest.

But what if it does work?

I think of how Logan stormed out of my apartment without looking back.

Am I ready to face him?

Every time I've thought about never seeing him again, this funny tightness would pinch in my chest, making me wonder if I was too young to have a heart attack, because it couldn't possibly be *feelings* causing it. Then I'd tell myself it was for the best.

But now that the opportunity might be right in front of me . . . I can't pass up the chance.

This probably deserves some kind of red alert. I'm not

ready to be done with a guy after one night.

Logan Brantley is unlike any man I've ever met before, so why am I surprised that he's the one to throw me completely off my game?

I let a scene play out in my head. What would happen if I showed up in Gold Haven, Kentucky, and walked into his repair shop? I can just picture the look on his face. *Shock.* But maybe excitement too?

But I'd have the upper hand, at least for a moment.

I make my decision as impulsively as I do everything else. If Greer's brother and sister-in-law say yes, I'm going to do it.

Banner Regent is packing up her shit (and vodka) and moving to Kentucky.

TWENTY

Logan

AS I PUSH MY CART DOWN THE AISLE OF PIGGLY Wiggly, I can feel eyes on me. My hands and clothes are clean, no trace of grease, but the scent of Fast Orange still clings. I nod to Mrs. Krispin, who works at the post office, and Ms. Cheadle, who works at the pharmacy.

Before I left town to join the corps, the manager would have been trailing after me to make sure I didn't shoplift, but today, eyes follow me for a completely different reason.

I stop in front of the meat case and pick up a couple of packages of steak. I'm checking out the marbling when Gloria Barnum pushes her cart up next to mine.

"I bet you've got some real talent with a grill."

I choose a package and meet her gaze. "I do all right. I'm sure there are people who do it better."

She scans the contents of my cart—a couple of dozen eggs, two pounds of bacon, orange juice, and a box of pancake mix. I haven't made it over to the lunch meat, bread, or beer yet.

"You trying to live on breakfast food, Logan Brantley?

Might need a touch of variety in your diet. My daughter Jessica makes a tasty bacon-stuffed chicken casserole. She grates her own cheese instead of using Velveeta, even though it melts faster. I know she'd love to make it for you some night."

Gloria's smile is as kind as her invitation, but I know what would happen if I accepted.

"That's a real nice thought, ma'am, but I'm a pretty simple guy and I can fend for myself. I'll get some potatoes to go with that steak. Maybe even some burger and buns, and I'll be set for a week."

She shakes her head, tsk-tsking quietly. "It's such a shame you have to cook every meal for yourself or go out. Jessica has to carry the whole load at her place now since that lowlife boyfriend of hers took off before the baby was even born. Give her a call sometime. I bet you'd both find it pretty nice to have someone to share a meal with now and again."

I wish I could say this is the first conversation I've had in Piggly Wiggly that jumped from talking about grilling to someone offering up their daughter, but it's not. I can't blame Gloria, though; she worries about her kid and grandbaby just like any decent mama would. It doesn't take a genius to figure out that an asshole who won't even stick around to see his kid born isn't likely to pitch in for support.

"I appreciate the struggle she's having, Gloria. It's a real shame. I'm sure she's going to find a great guy who will appreciate both her and that little girl."

She finally takes my hint that I'm not going to be that guy, and pushes her cart on down the aisle. I need a woman to want me for more than what I've got in my wallet or my bank account.

As I reach for a package of ground sirloin, I can't help but shake my head. It's funny how things change. Gloria Barnum would have had a heart attack if I'd pulled up in my Camaro to take Jessica on a date when I was in high school, and it wouldn't have been because of the three-year age difference.

The reputation I had as the troublemaking Brantley kid haunted me for years. Before I left the military, my mom passed away from a drug overdose, and when I came back to Gold Haven, people didn't exactly welcome me with open arms.

It wasn't until I took over Chuck's garage and word got out that I was making good money and keeping my nose clean that women started showing up at my service station with purposely flat tires and engines making funny noises only they could hear.

Mrs. Barnum disappears around the corner past the dairy case.

Which reminds me, I forgot to get cheese. After selecting some pepper jack, I grab lunch meat from the deli, bread, and a six-pack of beer.

I'm met with another familiar face when I push my cart into the checkout line. Unfortunately, this isn't a friendly one.

Roy Planter glares at me as his daughter, Rachel, sells him a case of beer and a carton of cigarettes. He leaves the stench of stale smoke behind him as he hands over the money. He keeps his scowl pinned in place as he hefts his purchases and leaves the store.

Rachel's expression isn't much different from her dad's.

"You know he needed that job."

I put my groceries on the belt and give her an answer she doesn't want to hear. "I needed your dad not to be drunk when he came into work to do that job."

The red blush of embarrassment stains her cheeks. "It's a disease, you know. How about a little Christian compassion? It ain't easy for him to deal with."

I reach for my wallet, amazed at her hypocrisy. "You ain't blaming this on me. You sell him a case of beer every damn day instead of pushing him to go to AA."

It sure isn't my place to judge, but if she's going to fault me for firing him after costing me thousands of dollars in damage, you better believe I'm going to point out her faults in return.

"He won't go to AA. I've tried. I don't know what else to do."

Her desperation comes through loud and clear, and I feel it to my depths. I felt the same way about my mama, and she was just as stubborn. I gave up on her, and maybe I shouldn't have. Rachel shouldn't make my mistake.

"Get your ma to push him too. It's not too late. Otherwise, one of these days he might not just hurt himself. He might hurt someone else, and this whole town would suffer for it."

An expression of despair creeps over her face, like she's already pictured the situation a hundred times. "I know," she whispers. "But Ma isn't going to do anything. She can't say a word without him flying off the handle."

"You ever heard of an intervention? Maybe you and your brother and your ma could all talk to him at the same time."

She shrugs, and I know the suggestion will go unused. She looks back up at me, pain in her eyes. "Want to help me forget about it for a few hours? I get off at ten."

When I came back to town, I promised myself I wouldn't be the guy with that reputation, the one who shits where he eats. I've done a pretty good job of staying true to that, and I'm not about to break the rule for Rachel Planter.

"Sorry, I've got plans."

She finally starts ringing up my groceries when I hear voices from the checkout lane beside me.

"Yep, she moved in today. I saw her. I guess Holly Wix is plannin' to use Rosemary's place as a flophouse for all her fancy New York friends."

Holly Wix, the hometown girl who made good, is the one who's ultimately responsible for me getting all tangled up with Banner. If Holly hadn't married a billionaire and his sister hadn't stayed at her gran's, I wouldn't know Banner existed.

And I wouldn't have left New York City with an empty flatbed and my pride shredded like the flag they just replaced outside the VFW.

"Who is it this time?" one woman asks.

"I'm not sure, but she was real pretty. Her hair was all different shades of blond. Must be some fancy new style. I wish I'd gotten a picture to show my niece. She'd know if it's someone famous."

No way in hell.

The description of "different shades of blond" doesn't seem too specific, but I know one woman who fits that description all too well.

But there's no way in hell Banner Regent would set foot

115

in BFE or Podunk or whatever else she called Gold Haven, Kentucky.

Unless she's here for you, a voice in my head argues.

I pay for my groceries, wish Rachel luck with her dad, and push my cart outside. I consider it fate that I'm parked next to Wanda Jenkins, who just delivered the gossip inside Piggly Wiggly.

"Can I give you a hand loading up your groceries, Ms. Jenkins?" I ask.

She's sliding her key into the trunk lock on her Bonneville, but pauses at my offer. "A handsome man who wants to help me with my bags? I'd be silly to say no."

I reach for a paper sack when she finishes unlocking and popping the trunk, and settle it inside. "Did you say there's someone staying at Holly's gran's place? I usually try to keep an eye on it, but I hadn't heard anything about someone coming to use it."

Ms. Jenkins's eyes light up at the prospect of her being *in the know* when clearly I'm not.

"Oh yes, that's exactly what I said. I saw her carrying a couple big suitcases inside, so maybe she's staying a while. But you know those city girls; they probably over-pack for every little thing."

"I do know a few of those city girls, and you're usually right. Maybe I should swing by and see what's going on there, just in case."

Her interest ticks up another notch. "You probably should. We need to look out for each other in this town. Outsiders aren't always welcome."

I hold back a sarcastic comment at her response, because even though I'm from this town, they all considered me an outsider until I started making bank.

"I'll report back with what I find."

She nods vigorously. "You be sure to do that."

Damn Holly and her friends, and all the trouble they've brought to my door.

I load my groceries into my truck, and when I pull out of the parking lot, I still turn in the opposite direction of home.

TWENTY-ONE

Logan

HOLLY'S GRAN'S HOUSE IS LIT UP. NOT JUST ONE light but all of them, like the person inside is scared of the dark. There's no car out front, but through the drawn lace curtains, I can make out a person inside.

I've got two choices: pick up the phone and call Holly to find out who's there, or knock on the door and find out for myself. I go for option two.

My headlights cut across the white siding and purple front porch. The curtains twitch, so I know whoever is inside knows they've got company.

I climb out of my truck, shut the door, and make my way up the front steps. When I knock on the door, the top of a blond head pops into view through the small glass windows set in the top of the door.

No fucking way. Turns out the gossips had it right this time.

She's not tall enough, so she has to jump to peek through the window. Her whiskey-colored eyes widen when she sees me.

"What the hell are you doing here, Bruce?" I call from the front porch when she disappears from view.

A few moments of silence pass before the door is yanked open and Banner Regent stares at me from behind the screen door.

"What the hell are *you* doing here?"

Banner cocks a jean-covered hip, and it's impossible to miss the attitude she's throwing my way. The chest area of her white sweater is smudged with dust, but she still looks downright edible. My cock takes notice, even though I tell myself I'm still pissed at her.

"What am *I* doing here? I live here. But last time I checked, New York princesses don't set foot in BFE."

Her full lips press into a flat line, but she still looks sexy as hell. *Fuck me.*

"First off," she says, raising one finger into the air, "I'm no princess. And if I were, you'd be wrong anyway, because I'm standing right in the middle of BFE."

"That doesn't answer my question."

"Does it matter?"

I grit my teeth. This woman is more frustrating than any I've met before, but damned if I don't like seeing her all riled up. "Sure does, especially if you're here to apologize for tossing me out of your apartment on my ass—"

She sucks in a breath. "I did not toss you out on your ass. You stormed out and left. Big difference, dude."

"That doesn't tell me why you're here."

She props a hand on her hip. "It's not really any of your business. I'm spending some time out of the city and doing a favor for a friend by housesitting."

I may have only spent one night with Banner, but I've

gotten to know her through weeks of texting. "What the hell happened?"

Her expression turns mulish. "Why do you think something happened?"

"Hell must have frozen over for you to leave your little universe of an island."

She cranes her head to the side to look behind me. "I don't see the devil ice skating behind you anywhere, so I guess you're wrong. Now, if you'll excuse me—"

A shrill beeping blares from inside.

"Shit!" Banner spins around and rushes back inside.

The unmistakable smell of smoke hits my nose, and I yank open the screen door. A gray cloud rises off whatever is on the stove as Banner grabs a towel and starts waving it around. She miscalculates her movements and the fringed ends catch fire.

"Fuck." I round the table that takes up the center of the kitchen and move her out of the way to turn off the burner and grab the towel out of her hand. Crossing the room, I toss it in the sink and put out the flames. I throw open the front windows before turning to face her.

"You trying to burn the whole damn house down?"

Her face pales to sheet white. "No."

The word comes out shaky, and it takes a shit load of willpower to stop myself from pulling her against my chest and holding her until the fright is forgotten. Instead, I scan the room to make sure nothing else is on fire as the smoke alarm finally quiets. My attention stops on the frying pan and what looks like charred roadkill inside it.

"I was trying to make dinner." Banner's tone starts out timid, but each word gains volume and sassy attitude.

"Until you showed up and started acting like a jerk and I burned it!"

She's so damn sexy when she's pissed. I can't help but push her a little more. "Honey, I think whatever you were making was doomed long before I showed up."

Her brows dive into angry slashes. "Why did I ever think I liked you? You're just as much of a jerk as those assholes in Manhattan."

I don't take offense to what I know isn't true. "At least I'm a jerk that doesn't burn dinner. What were you trying to make?"

She shakes her head. "Like you care."

I lean back, resting a hip on the table in the middle of the kitchen, and wait.

"Bacon. I was trying to cook bacon." She spits out the words, sounding so miserable, I almost feel bad for laughing at her.

"It's not the last pig on the planet, Bruce. No need to look like you're never gonna have bacon again."

"When you haven't had real bacon in approximately five years, it sure feels like it. That was the only package."

I look at the lump in the pan. "The whole package in one pan? Damn, Bruce. Did you separate it?"

She shakes her head. "I thought that happened as it thawed and cooked."

I'm pretty sure my eyebrows damn near hit my hairline. "You put frozen bacon in a chunk in a frying pan?"

Banner's shoulders slump as she lifts a hand to her face. "I knew I should have googled it. I don't cook, okay?"

"What'd you use that fancy kitchen in your apartment for then?"

"Heating up takeout. Caterers used it occasionally for dinner parties."

I'm not sure why I'm surprised, but I am. "Are you serious?"

"Does anyone deliver out here? Sushi? Thai? Vietnamese? I could go for some *pho*." She stops when she realizes what she just said is ridiculous, and holds up a hand. "Let me try that again. Pizza? Chinese?"

I'm already heading for the door when I answer. "There's one pizza joint in town that might deliver out this far, but even I wouldn't let you eat that."

TWENTY-TWO

Banner

"**Y**OU'RE JUST GOING TO LEAVE?"

First Logan Brantley shows up to see me murder bacon, and now he's going to just *leave* without another word?

"You really are an asshole," I yell as the door slams behind him.

I run to the screen to look out and see him pulling bags from his truck before making his way back to the front porch.

For some unknown reason, I don't hesitate to open the door to let him back inside. I tell myself it's because he's carrying grocery bags, and I'm so hungry I'd even eat a non-kosher hot dog.

Logan sets the bags on the table and turns around to meet my gaze. *Dammit. How is he even more freaking gorgeous than before? It's not fair.*

"You really shouldn't call the guy who's about to make you dinner an asshole."

His words send a shaft of shame through me. Why do I

keep screwing up when it comes to him?

"I thought you were just . . . leaving." It's on the tip of my tongue to apologize, but he interrupts me.

"You really don't know how to cook?"

I shake my head. "I'm from Manhattan. It's not a necessary skill."

"You're a long way from New York City, Bruce. How long are you staying, anyway? You still haven't told me why you're here."

I hate the fact that I have to tell him the truth. If anyone but Logan were standing in my kitchen, I'd stick with my *I just need a break from the city* line, but he already knows that's a lie.

"I don't know how long I'm staying."

He says nothing, clearly waiting for me to continue my explanation.

"Look, it's a long story, okay?"

With a nod, Logan turns and starts unloading the grocery bags on the table. "Then you can tell me while I cook, because you're not eating this bacon until I get a story that's free of bullshit."

My attention darts to the bags of groceries as a tingle of excitement takes root. "You have bacon in there?"

He glances over his broad shoulder, his muscles stretching against the shirt. "Sure do. That's what a real man buys when he goes to the store."

A real man. Like I need the reminder with how his presence sucks up the space in the small kitchen and makes it seem ten degrees hotter than the fire I almost started. *Only me . . .*

"If you want to run out to the truck, there's a six-pack

of beer too. Might as well crack some open."

"Bacon and beer. I guess real men don't mess around."

He shoots me a look that lights another kind of fire—this time between my legs. *No. Not going there.*

"We mess around plenty, just not about food."

Like I'm escaping the Texas chainsaw massacre, I rush toward the door and shut it behind me before I suck in a breath. *I can't be around him. It's not safe.* Pulling myself together, I pick my way along the uneven path to the truck and open the door.

The unique scent that clings to Logan Brantley wafts out—citrus and all things *man*. I tell myself it's not as sexy as it seems as I find the cardboard six-pack of bottles tipped over in the floorboard of the passenger side. One bottle rolled under the seat, so I pull it out.

A piece of paper sticks to a bottle.

If you're ever lonely, you know where to find me. 687-7896

Um. Excuse me?

I go to shove it back into the bowels of the truck where I pulled it from, but the crinkle of more paper stops me.

I should not be digging around in Logan Brantley's truck. Also, side note, I am not jealous.

I'm not. Seriously.

I pull out a handful of similar notes.

I'm available to make you dinner anytime.

Text me if you want me to cook the food you're inside buying. I know how to keep a man fed.

Bring your appetite over to my place and I'll fix you up.

If they were all in the same handwriting, I'd say Logan had a stalker, but the variety of names and numbers listed at the bottom of the notes reveal that's not the case.

Jesus, is every woman in this town throwing herself at Logan Brantley? And what is it with all the women who want to cook for him? Is it a Kentucky thing?

Seeds of jealousy take root inside me, and even though I try to stomp them out, they're pesky little assholes that won't take the hint.

So what if every single woman in this town thinks Logan Brantley is a catch? I wonder what they'd all think if they knew he drove almost a thousand miles to see me . . . and then stormed out of my apartment after our one-night stand.

Not even thinking about it.

I cram the notes back under the seat, grab the beer, and head back to the house. Even though I try to shut them down, two questions are front and center in my brain.

Does he take any of them up on their offers?

Why does he keep the notes?

When I slip back into the house, Logan has another frying pan on the stove. Thankfully, the mouthwatering scent of bacon has chased away the acrid stench of smoke.

He glances at me over his shoulder. "Thought you got kidnapped by Sasquatch or something."

"A bottle got stuck under the seat, and I got caught up reading your stash of dinner invitations."

His expression narrows, but I keep going.

"Do you ever have to cook for yourself? Or do you just

keep them all on rotation? Like, she does good chicken, her steak is better, but this one's casseroles are the shit, so I'm going to see her on comfort-food night."

"What makes you think I take any of them up on their offers?"

I set the beer on the table. "Why wouldn't you?"

Logan turns back to the frying pan. "Get the eggs out and whip up the pancake mix. If we're having bacon, we might as well have a full-blown breakfast."

Apparently that means the subject is closed. I don't want to keep it open either, so I pull the box of pancake mix out of the grocery bag and breathe a sigh of relief when it's one of those *just add water* kinds. Basically less chance of me screwing something else up tonight.

I open what seems like every cabinet door on my side of the kitchen without finding a bowl before I turn to Logan.

"Do you see any mixing bowls over there? I have no idea where anything is."

He flips a piece of bacon before opening a cabinet and pulling one out. I cross the room to take it from him, but he holds on.

"You think I would've fucked you in New York if I was fucking every woman in this town?" His words come out quietly, but with strength behind them.

I tug on the bowl, but he still doesn't let go. "I'm not asking for an explanation."

"And here I thought I gave you one before when I said I don't take everything that's offered. A lot of these women are looking for a man to provide, and I'm not taking the chance that I'll knock one of them up and get trapped into being a paycheck for eighteen years."

"And you weren't worried about knocking me up?" The question is out before I can take it back.

He shakes his head. "City girl like you, I figured you'd have your shit in order. And I always use a condom."

"City girl like me . . ." I try the words out. "You mean the slutty kind? The kind that likes one-night stands because they're easy, and I can get off and walk away without any complications?"

"I didn't say any of that."

"You didn't have to."

A heavy silence hangs over the kitchen, punctuated only by the popping of the bacon grease. Logan finally releases his hold on the mixing bowl, and I decide that I'm going to get drunk. *Surprise, surprise.*

I prepare the pancake mix on the opposite side of the kitchen, only approaching Logan to hand it off to him. As I reach for a beer, I see a container of orange juice peeking out from one of the bags. Well, hell, during the great mixing-bowl search, I found a bottle of vodka, and screwdrivers go better with breakfast than beer, in my opinion. I grab the orange juice and return to the cupboard for vodka to mix up my drink.

Logan snags a bottle of beer before he loads up another frying pan with pancakes.

"Want a screwdriver?" I ask, raising the vodka high.

He shakes his head as he pops the top off the beer and takes a swig. "No, what I want is the real story. So, get to it."

With my screwdriver in front of me, I settle into a chair and lean it back on two legs.

"The real story . . . I got fired from my job, evicted from my apartment, and when my parents wouldn't bother themselves to help and I couldn't bring myself to take a handout from a friend, this option came up, and I thought *what the hell.*"

Logan flips pancakes before glancing over his shoulder. "That's not exactly a long story."

"Maybe not, but those are the highlights."

"So coming here didn't have a thing to do with me."

I take a long drink of my screwdriver. Even now, with the warmth of vodka filtering through my body, I'm not sure how to answer that question.

I gesture in the direction of his truck with my glass. "You need another woman after you like I need another stroke of bad luck. Because, damn, that's a pretty impressive lineup of Suzy Homemakers looking to catch a man."

Logan steps away from the stove and meets my gaze for a long moment. "Maybe that's why I like you better. You're not looking for anything but a good time, and that's about all I've got in me right now."

His words sting more than I like to admit.

I'm the good-time girl. The party girl. The queen of one-night stands. I've embraced the title for the last ten years and earned every bit of it. But something about sitting here in a lilac-wallpapered kitchen with this man makes me wonder if it's time to try something different.

What the hell? Shut up, Banner. You're thinking crazy shit.

I take another quick sip, hoping it drowns out the strange feeling, but instead I zero in on Logan's ass and remember how big and perfect his cock was.

All the screwdrivers in the world won't stop the freight train of lust roaring through my veins. But maybe that's a good thing. Lust, I understand. So what if I just want to ride him like a bull?

Logan's deep drawl interrupts my thoughts. "You gonna make me bribe you with bacon to find out what put that look on your face?"

"I think the one-night-stand rule might need to be temporarily amended to allow a repeat," I blurt out.

"Is that so?" He turns back to the stove to finish cooking without a change in expression.

My patience for the day is shot, and so is my appetite for subtlety. "What does that mean?"

He reaches for his beer and sucks down a swig. "It means we'll see what happens. Now, get some plates. It's time to eat."

TWENTY-THREE

Logan

WOMEN ARE STRANGE AND UNIQUE CREATURES to begin with, but Banner is in her own league. When she bites into a crispy strip of bacon, the moan she lets out goes straight to my balls, reminding me of what she sounded like when she came on my fingers, mouth, and cock.

Is there any chance I'd turn down a second night with her? No way in hell. From the corner of my eye, I watch her eat as I finish cooking the eggs and then dump some onto both plates.

"It's probably a good thing you're not cooking for any of those women looking to tie you down, because they'd get a lot more creative if they knew you could whip this up so easily."

I laugh at her bluntness. "I'm pretty sure their breakfast-cooking skills are better than mine."

She lifts a piece of bacon into the air to gesture with it. "But you don't understand the appeal of watching a man cook. It's right up there with watching him come when you're on your knees between his legs."

I choke on my first bite of egg before my vision clouds with red at the thought of her getting another guy off. Something about Banner trips the trigger on my control. I don't fucking care how many guys she's been with, but I sure as shit don't want to hear about them.

"Then I guess you're going to have to drop to your knees in front of me and compare." I don't know where the words came from, but her eyes lift to mine and she blinks.

I like that shocked look on her face, the one she's probably more used to seeing on others, given her lack of filter.

Her surprise fades away just as fast, and Banner is back on her game. "Oh yeah, big boy? You think you could manage to stand and not let your legs give out?"

My cock presses so hard against the zipper of my jeans that it might leave a permanent mark, but I refuse to let her get the last word in.

"I'll stay standing even as I watch your throat work as you swallow every single drop."

Banner's eyes widen again, and a pink blush tinges her cheeks. I bet she didn't know she could blush anymore. The corners of my mouth tug with a smirk. I would never consider saying something like that to anyone else, but with Banner, it just sets her off.

She doesn't have a quick retort at the ready, so I keep pushing. "I bet if I slipped my hand in your panties right now, you'd be wet for me, wouldn't you?"

She shifts on her chair and reaches for her drink. She empties it in two big gulps before setting it back on the table in front of her. "I think I might need to go take them off."

The twinkle in her eye says she's sure she's tempting me.

But one thing I've learned with Banner is I have to work to keep the upper hand.

"Finish your food. Then you can go take them off."

She pushes her plate away. "I'm not hungry for this anymore."

"What are you hungry for, Banner?"

"I want that big cock in my mouth so I can remind you just how hard I can make you come."

Fuck . . . this woman.

"You think I forgot?" To myself I add, *No way in hell, Bruce.* I lean back and watch her face. "But a reminder wouldn't be unwelcome."

My taunt spurs her on. "You're also going to want pussy for dessert, so you better save room."

And I'm officially done. I drop my fork on the plate with a clang. "You're killin' me with that dirty mouth of yours."

"I may not be able to keep your stomach full, but I can keep your balls empty." Her lips turn up in a catlike smile. "So, what are you waiting for?"

"Fuck it." I rise from the table and take two steps to reach her side before lifting her off her chair.

I don't need directions to a bedroom in this house, so I head up the stairs with Banner's legs wrapped around my hips and her lips on my jaw.

When I get to the room Holly used as a kid, I lower Banner to her feet. She wastes no time going for my belt and pulling out my dick, only pausing when I pull her shirt up and over her head.

"Fuck, I missed your tits."

"I missed your cock."

A thought strikes me. "You better not be doing this

because you're drunk."

"Shut up, Logan. It was one screwdriver. At this point, you have to know I'd fuck you sober."

I wrap a hand around the back of her head and force her gaze to mine. "Goddamned right you will."

TWENTY-FOUR

Banner

LOGAN CRUSHES HIS MOUTH TO MINE AS I PALM HIS cock, and his groan vibrates against my lips. When I'm done with him, he's never going to forget tonight. And every time he thinks about one of those women making him dinner, he's going to remember how he got off after cooking for me.

I hate the jealousy that leaches into me like acid, but I can't help it. I've got something to prove. Maybe I'm only the good-time girl, but at least I know I'm fucking great at it.

I pull my lips away from his, and he tugs the shirt over his head. Trailing my tongue down his defined pecs and abs, I jack his cock the entire time. Logan's hand finally covers mine when I hit my knees.

Together, we stroke him to the edge of orgasm as I tease the head with my tongue and lips. I cup his balls in my free hand, and his growl of pleasure fills the room right before his balls pulse, and I swallow every single drop.

Logan's eyes open and he stares down at me on my

knees. "Jesus Christ, woman. You're fucking dangerous."

"We're not even close to done."

If sex is all we're going to have between us, then I'm going to make sure it's the best he's ever had.

"Give me a minute, and you're right—we're not done."

Before I realize what's happening, Logan has me on my knees on the bed, gripping the headboard behind me as I ride his face. His tongue lashes against my clit until I'm screaming his name and pressing hard against his lips.

He doesn't wait for my orgasm to subside before repositioning me on my hands and knees. I hear the tear of a wrapper before he pushes into me from behind.

I'll never admit it to him, but I love how he doesn't ask me what I want, and instead just gives me what I need.

"You're not done yet," he says. "You're gonna keep coming for me. You think I only want to hear you scream my name once? No fucking way. I want it again and again."

Logan's hand slides around my hip to cover my clit as he thrusts into me over and over. When he hits my G-spot perfectly and increases the pressure, I lose it. I'm a puddle on the bed by the time Logan yells out his own climax and collapses beside me.

Sleep pulls me under before I can even roll over.

TWENTY-FIVE

Banner

BRIGHT, BLINDING SUNLIGHT PIERCES MY EYES AND drags me out of sleep. I groan and try to roll over, but I'm pinned in the smallest bed I've ever slept in. *What the hell?*

Last night comes back in a rush. I'm in Gold Haven, Kentucky, in Holly's gran's house, and Logan Brantley's cock is pressed against my ass.

Jesus. Talk about a welcome celebration.

When I move, Logan jolts awake, sitting up.

"Fuck." He's out of bed and pulling on his jeans before I sit up.

"What?"

"I gotta get the hell out of here."

"Why? Are you late for something?"

"No, but I can't fucking be here right now." He throws on his shirt and is halfway out the door before I can ask my next question.

"Why not? What's the hurry?"

He doesn't answer because he's already stomping down

the stairs.

"What the fuck, Logan?"

Is this how he felt during our last morning after? For the record, it sucks.

I grab my jeans and shirt from last night and tug them on. By the time I hit the bottom of the stairs and step into the kitchen, Logan is reaching for the door handle.

"Really? Just like that? Is this how a *real man* handles the morning after in his hometown? What the hell is your problem?" I'm seething, and tempted to grab the nearest object and launch it at him.

"You don't fucking get it, do you?" he says.

"No, I really don't."

"This is a small town. Do you have any idea how many people probably already know I spent the night here? The gossip grapevine is alive and well, and within the next hour, everyone is gonna be talking about it. That's why I don't take any of those women up on their offers. I don't need to be the talk of the town. I've got a business to run, and that's all that matters to me."

His words carry a cold slap of reality.

I've been in this town for less than twenty-four hours, and apparently I'm already going to be labeled the Whore of Gold Haven. *Isn't that a fabulous way to start my new beginning?*

"I'm sorry to ruin Logan Brantley's perfect reputation. I didn't realize I'd be screwing you over while you were screwing me. I guess you better get out of here so you can salvage your public image."

He shakes his head, his hand still on the door knob. "You don't get it. But you will. You think Manhattan will chew someone up and spit them out? You've never lived in a small town."

"How bad can it possibly be to have a bunch of Betty Crocker wannabes turning up their countrified noses at me? I'm *so* concerned about their opinion." Sarcasm drips from my words like napalm, ready to ignite into rage at any moment.

Why did I think coming here was a good idea? Why did I think letting Logan inside this house, inside *me,* was a good idea? I could smack myself for letting it get this far out of hand.

Logan shakes his head. "I give you twenty-four hours before you're back on a plane to New York."

What. A. Dick.

"You know what? It's official. You're an asshole. Get the hell out."

When he opens his mouth, I don't want to know if he's going to deliver an apology or more angry words, so I hold up a hand. "Get out. Just get the fuck out."

Logan's mouth snaps shut and he's gone.

I drop onto one of the cushioned kitchen chairs, trying to figure out what just happened. I'm not sure I can handle more of this karma shit.

Last time, he was the one walking out with wounded pride, and now I'm surrounded by the tattered remains of mine.

Logan Brantley can take being a *real man* and shove it up his ass.

I spend the rest of the morning fuming and working

furiously on my laptop. My fledgling business doesn't stop just because some asshole doesn't want the people of this nowhere town to know he spent the night with me.

Three hours pass before I stand and stretch, amazed that I accomplished so much in such a short period of time. My stomach rumbles, reminding me that I'm starving. Logan's groceries are in the fridge, but there's no way I'm touching them.

Even if I knew what to do with a steak, I wouldn't eat it.

I check the time again; my rental car should be here any moment. Holly and Crey insisted on paying for one since I wouldn't take any money for "house-sitting." I have my pride, and no one is going to pay me for squatting my homeless ass here.

Opening the fridge again, I decide that the orange juice inside is fair game. I basically claimed it as mine last night.

There's a knock at the door at noon, and I peek through the lace curtains to see who it is. Two cars are parked out front, and a man is still sitting in the running one. *Perfect.*

I unlock the ancient dead bolt and pull the door open.

"Ms. Regent?" the man at the door asks.

"Yes."

He holds out a set of keys. "This is yours for however long you need it. Just call the number on the key tag to give us the location when you want us to come pick it up."

That's easy.

"Thank you," I say as I accept the keys, and he turns and heads back to the other car.

And just like that, I've got wheels, which means it's time to shower so I don't actually look homeless while I explore Gold Haven.

TWENTY-SIX

Logan

I DON'T HEAR THE DING OF THE DOOR CHIME OVER MY music, but as soon as someone turns Black Sabbath down, I know I have a visitor. Unfortunately, both of my employees are taking a smoke break, so I slide my creeper from under the car I'm working on and look up.

Julianne props a hand on her cocked hip and stares down at me. "Well, well. Aren't you the talk of the town this morning. I knew that bad boy from high school was hiding somewhere inside the upstanding-citizen thing you've got going on these days."

Even though I expected this, it's not what I want to hear. "How bad is it?"

"The girls at the salon have been buzzing about it all mornin'. Lots of speculation on the woman, that's for sure. Some are saying that Holly Wix ran away from her husband, and you're her secret lover."

"You've gotta be fucking kidding me." I stand up and wipe my hands with a rag from my back pocket.

"Nope, not at all. I'm sure that'll probably make the

tabloids, because I know for a fact that Deana has pictures of your truck out front of Holly's gran's house, and will probably try to sell them because her ex is seven months late on child support and she's getting desperate."

"Fuck. I better call Holly and give her a heads-up."

"That might be smart."

"What else?" I ask.

"Your favorite restaurant manager stopped in to get a nail fixed and got the whole story from the peanut gallery. If you're looking to make any moves there, you might have to do some damage control."

I don't owe Emmy any explanations, but that isn't something I need to tell Julianne, because it'll just add to the gossip mill that's already churning.

"Anything else?"

"That's about it, but for sure when whoever you were fucking all night long makes an appearance, she's gonna get the side-eye like nobody's business. So you might want to make sure she's aware of what's coming too. Unless it was a *wham, bam, thank you, ma'am* kinda thing."

I know this is Julianne's way of trying to find out exactly who's staying at Holly's gran's house, and my answer will set the tone for how the entire town treats Banner for as long as she's here.

I choose my words carefully. "When it comes out, you can tell anyone who says a cross word to her or about her that they'll answer to me."

"So that's how it is?" Julianne drawls.

"That's how it is."

"Ain't that an interesting piece of information? So it's serious between you two?"

I give her a hard look as I remember the blowout Banner and I had this morning. "That's not up for discussion."

"But you know this whole town is gonna speculate on it anyway."

"They can go ahead and speculate all they want. I don't care. But if anyone says—"

Julianne finishes my sentence. "One cross word to this mystery woman, you're going to be knocking it back down their throats." She tilts her head to the side. "You know that's not gonna stop it."

"It should help."

Julianne laughs and turns for the door. "I guess we'll see." She pauses at the threshold that leads from the garage into the waiting room. "By the way, you need a haircut. I can fit you in tonight after I close up, if you're still here."

I nod. "I'll let you know. Thanks."

I pull out my cell phone as soon as she's out the door to call Holly. I get her voice mail, so I leave her a message. Here's hoping she and her husband—who isn't my biggest fan, for the record—thinks this whole mess is funny.

Three hours later, I'm about to lock the doors of my shop so I can get some work done. I've had more casual visitors wanting to make appointments and shoot the shit than I can count on one hand. They're all not-so-subtly probing for information.

"So, you've got a friend in town?"

"I hear you're keeping some late hours."

I still haven't heard back from Holly, and I've stopped myself from texting Banner all day. I was a dick this morning, and I know it. But realizing how badly I fucked up by leaving my truck parked out front all night set me off.

In a small town, you've got one chance to make a first impression. I know how hard it is to change that impression, and what people are gonna be saying about Banner pisses me off already. The double standard is alive and well, and even more pronounced here. She'll be branded a slut before she even steps foot out of the house, and it's all my fucking fault. I shouldn't have said what I said, and I need to apologize, but I'm not sure I'll be able to get within firing range of her.

I finally give in to the urge and pick up my phone to text her.

LOGAN: *I'm sorry about this morning. I'd like to deliver the apology and explanation in person.*

TWENTY-SEVEN

Banner

WHOEVER PERPETUATED THE HOLLYWOOD IDEAL that small towns are friendly and welcoming is full of shit.

Everywhere I've gone today, which isn't many places because there aren't many to go, has been filled with people looking at me like I'm some kind of hooker. And that's without wearing anything flashy or scandalous. Skinny jeans, heeled boots, and a long pale blue sweater make up my outfit, but the women in this town are eyeing me like I'm walking around in stripper heels and a G-string.

I'm in the grocery store, searching the shelves high and low for organic, non-GMO steel-cut oats, when I finally overhear some of the snide comments that I'm sure have been making the rounds all morning.

"I heard she lured Logan Brantley there by saying it was Holly Wix, and we all know that he's had a thing for Holly forever."

"Oh, I bet you're right, Tricia. Otherwise, he would've already put a ring on Emmy Harris's finger. How long can

145

Logan possibly carry a torch for Holly? She's married to that billionaire guy now."

A third voice joins the conversation. "There's no way he's carrying a torch for Holly still if he's banging some New York skank friend of hers. Besides, I heard he told Julianne from Cut a Bitch that he'll be handling it personally if he hears anyone say a cross word about this mystery woman."

The first voice replies. "He can handle me personally anytime. I know my way around a man."

"Hasn't it been like ten years since you've had a real man in your bed? Leave it to someone who doesn't need pruning shears to be ready for him."

Wow. These bitches take no prisoners. My curiosity is stronger than my shame, though, because I want to see exactly who's talking shit about me so I don't accidentally end up being nice to them later.

I push my cart around the end of the aisle in their direction, and sure enough, there they are. A brassy blonde who desperately needs a better colorist, a brunette, and a woman with salt-and-pepper hair in short curls. All three heads swing in my direction as the wheels of my cart squeak.

"I don't mean to interrupt your gossip free-for-all, but do you know if there's a non-GMO or organic section in this grocery store? This New York skank has some standards."

Two faces pale, as expected when caught in the middle of an epic gossip session, but the brassy blonde straightens her shoulders.

"You'll probably want to go back to New York for that. Here we just have normal-people food and none of that fancy crap."

"I'm not leaving anytime soon, so I guess I'll have to

ask Logan to help me find what I need."

All their eyes widen at the mention of his name.

"It sounds like he already found what you needed," the blonde says in a snotty tone.

"My G-spot, my clit, and the back of my throat? Absolutely." With a smile, I turn my cart around and push it in the opposite direction.

Churn that through the gossip mill, bitches. See if I care.

On the way to the checkout, I grab a bag of Doritos and a fifth of Fireball.

Contrary to what my parents and probably the rest of the people who know me think, I do work hard. I just never let anyone see that side of things. Why? Because they would laugh me off as being ridiculous if they knew about my current project.

Screw the haters, because I'm going to be a success on my own terms.

I work at the kitchen table until my phone is nearing the end of its battery life, so I have to stand and stretch and go dig out the charger to keep my Internet hotspot going. If I'm going to stay here long term, I need to look into getting Internet service.

Four hours of conference calls later, and I'm done working for the day. There's always more I can do, but my eyes are bleary from staring at the computer screen all day, and my mind has hit the wall.

Before I got on the phone, I gave in and responded to Logan, but I've received zero response to my *when and where* text.

Maybe he changed his mind?

As much as I would like to think I do, I don't know Logan that well. A couple of weeks of texting, even if we were at it nearly around the clock, doesn't add up to knowing how a person is going to react to you showing up in his hometown and saying you're going to stay a while.

Maybe we need a fresh start. Maybe it's my turn to find him and offer the olive branch. I close my laptop and go upstairs to change and touch up my makeup before heading out to my rental car.

Thirty minutes later, I'm driving around Gold Haven like a freaking stalker. There's not even an actual stoplight in this town, only a blinking light. When I pull up to it in front of Logan's shop and see all his lights are off, my stomach sinks.

I've still gotten zero response to my text, and I have no idea where he lives, so that's out of the question. It's after eight, and I don't know where else to look. I take a left at the blinking light, and that's when I see his truck still parked around the side of his shop, but again, no sign of life inside.

It only takes one swivel of my head to the right to figure out exactly where he's at—the salon across the street. Through the well-lit window, I see Logan in the stylist's chair, cape wrapped around his neck. A woman holds her clippers above his head as he throws it back in laughter. She's laughing too. Logan's hand slips out from under the cape to wipe at what must be a tear in his eye, and the woman makes a similar movement.

The scene seems to play out in slow motion as I drive away, finally turning my head to stare at the road in front of me.

The reminder hits me hard.

This is Logan's world. This town is filled with his people. And I don't fit in.

The realizations continue to batter me as I brake at the stop sign just ahead before turning back toward my temporary home.

I don't belong here.

I don't belong anywhere.

TWENTY-EIGHT

Banner

THE PITY PARTY IN MY RENTAL CAR IS REACHING pathetic levels as I pull back into the gravel drive of Holly's gran's house and drop my forehead against the steering wheel.

"What now?" I whisper to absolutely no one.

At least at home, I could walk across the hall and be treated to unsolicited advice from Frau Frances. Even though the woman outed me to the association board, I actually miss her.

Before I can talk myself out of it, I grab my phone, pull up her contact information, and call.

"Frances residence."

Recognizing the voice of Irene, one of her caretakers, I say, "This is Banner Regent. I could feel Myrna missing me all the way from New York."

"Ms. Regent, it's good to hear from you. Let me see if Mrs. Frances is available to speak with you."

I roll my eyes. "We both know she's going to say no, even though she wants to say yes. Tell her it's Smith

College wanting to discuss naming a building after her."

A few beats of silence pass before Irene replies. "I'm going to tell her you lied to me, you know."

A chuckle rises up from my chest, already lightening my mood. "Perfect."

"Hold, please."

I wait sixty seconds before Myrna's familiar raspy voice comes through.

"I'm not giving you any more damn money, if that's what you're asking."

My lips stretch in a smile. "Color me shocked, Myrna. And here I thought you were going to give me all your millions after I was evicted."

"Who is this? Because you sound like that ungrateful girl who used to live across the hall from me."

"The one and only. You know you've missed me. Come on . . . you can admit it."

"Please tell me you're not homeless and hooking on the street."

That pulls a full-blown laugh from me. "I'm really not. I'm in Kentucky, trying on the small-town life." That should knock her back in her rocking chair. I didn't tell Frau Frances where I was going before I left New York, because I was still pissed at her for tattling on me to the board.

"Kentucky?" The shock in her voice comes through loud and clear. "Why in God's name would you go there?"

"I needed a cheap place to live so I don't end up homeless and hooking," I say, throwing her words back at her.

"Do they even fluorinate their water? It can't be

remotely civilized. You'll probably get eaten by some strange animal."

I'm not sure Myrna has left New York in twenty years, so her priceless reaction is just the comic relief I needed.

"So far the only thing that's been eaten is my—"

She cuts me off before I can finish. "Gah! Still haven't learned to keep your legs closed, you—"

Laughter bursts from my lips, drowning out whatever she says next, which is probably for the best. I wipe the tears from my eyes with the sides of my fingers so I don't smear my eyeliner.

"Thank you, Myrna, for giving me exactly what I needed. You don't have to admit it, but I know you miss me."

She harrumphs, and it's almost as good through the phone as in person. "If I did miss you, it's only because the couple who moved in across the hall have a fondness for curry, and I'm choking to death on air freshener to get rid of the smell. If I die from this, I'm blaming you."

Surprisingly, I don't actually want to argue that it's her own fault she's stuck with the scent of curry.

"Good night, Myrna. I hope you wake up tomorrow."

"If you feel the urge to bother me again, do it at a decent hour."

The phone clicks, and I'm left with a small smile on my face. I really do miss the old lady. I always know how she's going to treat me, because she never veers from it.

Unlike Logan lately.

My smile fades away, and I give myself a mental slap for thinking about him. What I need is another distraction. One that serves alcohol.

Greer said there is a bowling alley within walking distance from here. A hike, but walkable. I shift the car in reverse, determination rising to the surface.

It's time to see what Gold Haven has to offer in the way of distractions.

TWENTY-NINE

Banner

THE NEON SIGN SAYS PINTS AND PINS, BUT THE *N* IN PINTS is unlit, so it reads PI TS AND PINS. Considering the peeling paint on the outside of the building and the rutted gravel parking lot, this place has definitely seen better days.

But beggars can't be choosers, and this is the top of my list of options, especially because it seems to be the only thing open in this town. I'm not going back to that hair salon to knock on the window and ask Logan to keep me occupied tonight, that's for damn sure.

As I walk inside, I wonder if my skinny jeans and even skinnier heels are a bad choice. You can see through my long black blouse to the black lacy cami beneath. In New York, I would have gone more scandalous, wearing only a bra under it, but I don't want to cause any heart attacks in this town. From the looks I'm getting as I walk in the door, apparently my idea of conservative and Gold Haven's idea of conservative are two different things.

The curious eyes scanning me from head to toe belong

to both men and women, but I don't slow my stride. I go directly to the bar. A woman is singing karaoke on a small stage, and I'm reminded that this is where Holly Wix got her start. *Quaint.*

"You look like trouble," the bartender tells me.

She's a heck of a lot tougher looking than I am . . . or maybe that's just the impression her scar gives off. It starts at her jaw and wraps around to the opposite side of the base of her throat. Her dark hair is pulled away from her face in a bun, but not a messy, sexy one you might see on a bartender in Manhattan. Hers is tight and no nonsense.

I meet her direct stare. "I'm really not that much trouble."

She sets a shot glass on the old wooden bar in front of me, scans me from head to toe, and then turns to grab a bottle of Ketel One from the top shelf. She pours the shot and slides it toward me.

"What's this for?"

"It's not on the house, if that's what you're thinking. That shit comes out of my paycheck, which is a joke to begin with."

"So why would you give me something I didn't order?"

"You were going to order some kind of fancy vodka cocktail that I don't have the patience to google, so I'm cutting out all the time we would waste going through that song and dance."

Surprisingly, I like her gruff, take-no-shit attitude, but that doesn't mean I'm going to let her think she knows anything about me.

"What is it with bartenders thinking they know everything? I mean, I could've come in here looking for a cold beer."

She shakes her head, and her brown eyes meet mine. "You're so full of shit. I'd bet all my tips tonight that you never order beer."

I think about ordering one just to prove her wrong, but it's a waste of posturing. "You're right. I wouldn't."

I pick up the shot glass and pour the vodka down my throat. The burn and then the warmth it leaves in its wake both give me the distraction I'm needing tonight.

"Another?" she asks.

"You're not going to assume?"

She gives me a single shake of her head. "Nah. That party trick only works once." She wipes off her hands with the bar rag and holds one out to me. "I'm Nicole."

I shake her hand and realize it's one of the only sincere greetings I've gotten in this town. "Banner."

Her eyes widen. "No shit? I've already heard of you."

I push the shot glass across the bar toward her. "You better pour me another."

She reaches to refill the shot. "You're the one from up north that apparently rode Logan Brantley's dick all last night."

I choke on the liquor as I toss it back. Her lack of filter reminds me of me.

"You pay a lot of attention to gossip?" I ask when I'm done coughing.

"I can't avoid it, working behind this bar. But that's only part time. I work swing shift at the furniture factory too. I pick up as much extra work as I can, including sometimes changing oil for Logan at the garage when he needs an extra set of hands."

An older man sidles up to the bar wearing a VFW trucker hat, a flannel shirt, and wrinkled black slacks. "I need another beer, Nicole, and Rosie is MIA."

"Sorry, Joe. Her kid's been sick lately, so she's had to leave a lot. I'll fix ya right up." She pulls a pint glass from behind the bar and slides it under the tap.

The old man takes the stool next to mine, but ignores me completely. "So you heard about the house that blew up on County Line Road tonight? It was next to Millie Freeman's place, and she's raising a stink. Cops can't keep ignoring this shit much longer, because Millie ain't having it."

"Another meth house?" Nicole asks.

"That's what they're saying."

"Such a shame. We keep losing employees here and at the factory because they come in high as a kite, tweaking, and can't barely string five words together."

Joe nods. "Same everywhere. I swear, it's a damned epidemic. Someone's getting rich off it while they poison this town."

"Do the police have any leads?" I ask, interjecting myself into the conversation.

"Who the hell are you?" Joe asks, swinging his head toward me.

I hold out a hand. "Banner Regent. I'm new in town."

Old Joe looks me up and down. "Shit, I can tell you're not from here. What the hell brings you to Gold Haven?"

Isn't that the million-dollar question?

"I think she's here to lock down Logan Brantley," Nicole offers.

I cut my gaze to her. "Really? You're just going to throw

me under the bus like that? And by the way, I'm not here to lock anyone down. I needed a change of place and a change of pace. I'm friends with Holly Wix's sister-in-law, so she let me use the house in exchange for keeping an eye on it."

Joe accepts my explanation at face value and nods. "It's a good thing, because I think these meth houses that've been blowing up are usually vacant or abandoned. It would've been terrible to see Rosemary's place go up next."

That thought, while horrible, actually makes me feel a little better about this whole deal. Maybe I really am offering a useful service to Holly and Creighton.

"That would be a shame," Nicole says, setting the beer in front of Joe.

"Damn right. Fuckin' tweakers don't have a single thought in their head to the damage they're causing." He leans forward and whispers to Nicole. "But the cops don't think it's possible that it's just a few random individuals cooking this shit. There's too much of that shit moving around this town, from what I overheard."

"What does that mean?" I ask.

Nicole answers instead of Joe. "It means we've got someone in this town running a drug operation while they're living right under our noses."

"Shit's gonna get bad if we start pointing fingers at each other," Joe says.

She nods. "I suppose that's best left up to the cops to figure out before people start throwing accusations around."

"Things are bound to get messy either way, in my opinion. Not that anyone gives a shit what this old man has to say."

Nicole wipes the towel along the bar again, covering

the same spot for the third time. "You better not get shit messy in here, old man."

Joe takes his glass with a jerk of his chin and heads back to a table filled with men his own age, all sporting hats with names of various ships or VFW posts on them. Several canes lean against the edge of the table.

Nicole follows my gaze. "VFW is closed today, so the whole crew shows up here. It's a regular thing."

As soon as she finishes explaining, one of the old men gets up for his turn at karaoke and begins to belt out "Proud to Be an American," and I can't help but smile. *This* is more along the lines what I figured Small Town, USA, would be like. Like a John Mellencamp song.

"So, you want another shot, or are you going to make me google some fancy shit?"

I smile. "What if I just make it myself? I'm not a half-bad bartender. It was my night gig in college."

Nicole rears her head back. "College girl *worked*?"

"Shocking, right? I needed money to pay rent and party after my parents cut me off. I got really good at slinging cocktails and getting tips." I look at her man's work shirt buttoned all the way to the top. "You said you're always picking up extra shifts for cash? What if I could teach you how to maximize the shifts you've got here?"

She gives me a skeptical look. "You want to work the bar in a bowling alley to teach me how to make more money?"

"Is your boss going to care? You're short a pair of hands, right?"

Nicole glances in what I assume is the direction of the office. "He's only going to care if you show up asking to get paid."

"Nah. But I'm keeping my own tips."

The door to the bowling alley opens, and Nicole's attention swings toward the group of six guys walking in.

"Shit. I'm going to need all the help I can get."

I reach for the top button of my blouse and undo all of them before shimmying it off. "Is there somewhere I can put this where it won't get dirty? There's no way I'm trusting it to any dry cleaner here if it gets beer on it."

She takes it from me and opens a cupboard where I see a purse stashed. "This good?"

"That'll work."

I hand her my tiny clutch too, and she tucks it inside. I make quick work of my own drink and suck it down while the men put in orders for food at the window across the way from the bar.

"I'll play cocktail waitress while you watch and learn. These skills are just as easy to implement behind the bar, I promise."

"I'll believe it when I see it."

I throw her a wink and get to work. The skills I honed in college come back as soon as I take my first order.

THIRTY

Logan

AFTER I FINISH WITH MY HAIRCUT FROM JULIANNE, I head home to shower and change into something that doesn't smell like my shop.

I sent a reply to Banner as I left the house, telling her to meet me at Pints and Pins so we can talk, but I've gotten no answer. I drove past Holly's gran's place on the way here, and it was dark, so maybe Banner beat me here. The parking lot is packed, which usually never happens unless Holly is in town singing, or the state bowling tournament quarter-finals are going on.

Holly hasn't been back in a while, and I know there's no tournament tonight. So, what the hell is going on to draw such a crowd?

I walk inside and stop just beyond the door.

You've gotta be fucking kidding me.

The scene in front of me gives me an idea of how Creighton Karas felt when he walked into this place and saw his wife entertaining an entire room.

Except Banner isn't singing. She's holding everyone's

attention captive just by existing—and apparently serving drinks.

I see Ben shuffle out of his office. "You make a new hire, old man?"

Ben has owned this place for as long as I can remember, but the last few years have taken a heavy toll on him. Rumors are floating around that his health is going downhill fast, and he's been making inquiries into selling the bowling alley but hasn't found any takers. Very few people in this town have enough money to cover all their own expenses every month, let alone buy an established business that requires a good deal of cash flow to keep it running. Even I don't have that kind of capital right now, and God knows I'm not looking to borrow more from the bank.

Ben follows my gaze to the bar area, and we both watch as Banner flits from table to table, taking orders and delivering drinks.

"She sure livens up the place, doesn't she?"

"You hire her?" I ask again.

He shakes his head. "Nah, she's one of Holly's friends from New York City, and said she'd help out for the night if she could keep her tips. Nicole was getting behind after Rosie left to take care of her kid, so it wasn't like I could say no. Word must've gotten around, because I haven't seen this place this packed since Holly was here last. Shit, I might actually have to try to hire her."

No way in fucking hell. The words echo in my head, but I keep them from springing free. "Banner's just having some fun. She's not staying long, and even if she were, I don't think she's the type to work a job like this for real."

We both continue to watch her, and Ben replies, "She

said she waitressed and bartended for four years of college in bars and clubs in New York, so I think you're wrong about that. She's got the knack for it, and shit, even the crankiest of the VFW crew is half in love with her already."

The knowledge that Banner actually worked her way through college surprises me, and maybe that makes me an asshole for assuming she sponged off her mommy and daddy.

What else don't I know about her?

I don't have any time to ponder the answer to that question because I see Rusty Mills grab Banner around the waist and pull her down on his lap. He's a piece of shit for a lot of reasons, and not just because he faked a back injury to collect disability from the state. Asshole has a nicer truck than I do, and he hasn't worked a day in the last year.

When I charge forward, Ben calls after me, "You do any damage, you're paying for it."

Fuck it.

But I don't get there quick enough, because Rusty's already got his lips planted on hers. The whole table of his drunk buddies is cheering, but all I see is red.

I lunge for Banner, but she's one step ahead of me as Rusty rips his mouth away.

"Whoa there, darlin'. You just let go of those right now, and we'll call it no harm, no foul."

Banner's hand is planted in the crotch of Rusty's loose jeans, and his words clue me in to exactly what's happening—she has him by the balls.

"I've been friendly, Rusty. I've laughed at your jokes, brought you your beers, even refilled the bar mix three times because you're a big fan of that shit. I didn't put a stiletto through your work boot the first time you 'accidentally' grabbed my ass. I didn't even poison your drink when you made a comment about my tits as I walked away last time. But a girl has to draw the line somewhere."

Rusty's face turns even redder, and he lets out a squeak as Banner twists her arm sideways.

"So this line I mentioned, it's where you apologize and tell me you're never going to put your hands on another woman without her permission. Does that make sense? Am I being clear enough for you, Rusty?"

He squeaks again and nods his head vigorously. "I swear I won't. Oh my God, you're going to crush my nuts. Please let go."

"I didn't hear an apology," Banner says with a sweet smile, and the whole table of men around her laugh as Rusty's face turns a deeper shade of red.

"I'm sorry. I'm so fucking sorry. Please let go."

Banner releases her hold and jumps off his lap. Rusty bolts up so fast, the chair tips over as he falls to his knees.

She pitches her voice sweetly and says, "That's too precious that you want to pray about what you just did. That instant repentance must be a Southern thing."

A roar of laughter comes from Rusty's friends, and I'm pretty sure no one in this bar will let him live tonight down. Banner probably just became some kind of local celebrity, because Rusty's been known to have wandering hands on more than one occasion, but no woman has ever put him in his place quite so effectively.

Banner tips Rusty's chair back up and steps onto the seat in her heeled boots. She surveys everyone in the bar except me, because I'm behind her.

"Anyone else have any questions about whether I want you grabbing my ass or trying to kiss me while I bring you your drinks?"

"No, ma'am." The shouts go up.

She might not realize it, but Banner has officially been accepted by the town, and I'm damn proud of her for the way she handled herself.

I didn't have to see that to know she's one hell of a woman. I'd have to be an idiot not to keep Banner Regent in my life for as long as she'll let me.

"Good. Right. So everyone understands they'll be keeping their hands to themselves from now on?"

"I'm sorry, but I've got a problem with that," I call out, and Banner glances over her shoulder at me.

"Is that right?"

"Yeah, that's right." I stalk forward and lift her off the chair. "If you haven't already heard the gossip, I've got a pretty powerful need to have my hands on you."

My declaration sends the crowd into another roar.

Banner's eyes widen. "And here I thought you didn't want anyone to know about that little problem of yours."

Everyone in the bar quiets to hear us.

"It's only a problem if I can't have the woman I want."

"I guess you're going to have to wait and see what she wants." Banner pushes out of my arms to land on her own two feet.

"I know what she wants, but we're both too hardheaded sometimes."

"Hardheaded? Is that another way of saying you were an asshole?" she asks as she turns away to walk toward the bar and pick up another round of drinks.

I follow her. "Yes. I was an asshole, and I'm apologizing for it."

"Is that why you couldn't manage to reply to me all damned day?"

The vehemence in her tone takes me by surprise, but instead of following her again, Nicole distracts me.

"You have any fucking clue what you just did?" she asks.

"What are you talking about?"

"This whole town thinks you and Emmy Harris are going to end up getting married and having babies, and you just told an entire bar full of people that you're after this girl from New York. The gossips are going to have a field day with that."

I didn't exactly think about my words before I spoke them, but I'm not taking them back. Do I feel bad that Emmy is going to hear it secondhand from someone else approximately five minutes from now? Yes. She's a good woman, and she deserves to hear it from me that my interests lie elsewhere.

Nicole is filling pint glasses under the tap and waiting for an answer.

"It's not like I planned this."

She raises an eyebrow. "When does a man ever plan anything?"

Banner returns with an empty tray and reaches over the bar to grab a cocktail and take a sip. "I'm not leaving until this crowd clears out, so you can either wait or we can talk tomorrow."

"Since when do you work here? And if you work here, why the hell are you drinking on the job?"

"Who would work here without perks?" Nicole lifts a shot glass to catch my attention and tosses it back.

Banner jerks her head toward Nicole. "What she said."

"Then I guess you better get me a Coke, because if you're drinking, I'm driving you home."

Banner cocks a hip and stares me down. "You think I can't get myself home?"

"I think it's a miracle that you even know how to drive after living in New York your whole life."

"I drove outside the city sometimes."

"Either way, you're not a regular behind the wheel, and the last thing I want is to see you wrapped around a tree somewhere because neither your skills nor your reaction time is up to par."

"Listen to the man. He's not an idiot all the time." Nicole points at her throat. "Besides, an asshole drunk driver ran me off the road on my bike a couple years back, and I got tangled up in a barbed-wire fence. I thought I was going to bleed out right there, but the asshole's fucking OnStar shit automatically called 911 and an ambulance came. So basically the driver almost killed me and saved my life at the same time. Don't be that guy."

Nicole's story has a sobering effect on Banner, who pushes the rest of her cocktail away. "I'm officially done drinking. Maybe forever. Jesus. If y'all just had cabs or public transportation, everyone could drink and get home safely."

I can't help but laugh. "Y'all? You're saying y'all now?"

Banner narrows her eyes at me. "I'm trying it out."

"Try it out all you want. I'll be waiting right here. We've got a hell of a lot to talk about."

I'm right about at least one thing tonight—Banner won over a chunk of the townspeople, and as she works the room and delivers drinks to the stragglers who aren't yet ready to go home, Ben finds me at the bar and takes a seat.

"You think that city girl has enough money to buy me out?"

Nicole freezes with her hands in the sink. "You said you'd sell this place to me."

He nods at her, but it's dismissive. "How are you ever going to get that much money, Nicki? You're hustling your ass off everywhere you can, but I can't afford to finance the sale of this place and let you pay me off over a few years. I need a lump sum from someone so I can retire and not worry about it going under and losing my retirement fund."

"It wouldn't go under."

I hate that I'm caught in the middle of this discussion, but there's no easy way to extricate myself from it other than to mention one thing.

"I don't think Banner's looking for this kind of investment. She's got her own stuff going on." To myself, I add *that she hasn't even told me details about.*

Ben looks from me to Nicole, who I know he'd love to see take over Brews and Balls, which is what the locals call Pints and Pins, but unfortunately he doesn't have the means to just give it to her.

"I guess it's good to know where we all stand," Ben says awkwardly before he slides off his stool and shuffles toward the office.

Nicole watches him leave. "He's never going to believe

I can raise enough money to buy this place, but goddammit, I will. I can't spend the rest of my life working in that factory."

Determination takes over her expression as Banner steps up beside me. "What's with all the serious faces? What did I miss?"

Nicole looks down at the glasses in the sink. "Nothing important."

THIRTY-ONE

Logan

I T'S ALMOST TWO O'CLOCK BY THE TIME I FINALLY DRAG Banner out of the bowling alley. She decided that since I wasn't letting her drive either way, she might as well have another drink with Nicole. It was almost like she could tell Ben had just crushed the girl's dream, even if she wasn't present for the conversation. But given how long Banner dragged it out, I have to wonder if she was trying to avoid leaving.

I lift her up into the passenger side of the truck and shut the door before heading around to climb into the driver's seat.

"You afraid to be alone with me now?" I ask her.

"No. Of course not."

"Then what's going on?"

Banner stares down at her hands in her lap. "This morning sucked balls, and now all of a sudden you don't care if people know you've got a thing for me. I can't keep up with you. I get that this is your town and I don't fit in here. Trust me, that was very clear today at the grocery store."

"You don't think you made some headway on that tonight? Half the town was in that bar, and they're on your side."

Banner shakes her head. "The male half. That's not the problem. All the women still think I'm some big-city skank coming to steal one of their prime men, and they have no problem showing it."

"What happened?"

When Banner fills me in on her grocery store experience, I try to hold back my laughter, but it's a lost cause.

"Your G-spot, your clit, and the back of your throat? I wish I could've seen their faces when you said that."

She glares at me from the passenger seat. "At least now they know I'm a skank for sure, and they don't have to gossip about it."

I come to a stop at the edge of the bowling alley parking lot and give her a hard look. "You keep referring to yourself as a skank, and we're going to have a hell of a problem."

"Why's that?"

"Because you're probably going to be pissed when I put this truck in park and drag you over my lap to spank some sense into your ass."

Her eyes widen with shock. "You wouldn't."

I tilt my head to the side. "Wouldn't I? No one gets to talk shit about you around me, including you, and I'll do what it takes to make sure you understand that."

When she goes quiet, I have a choice to make. I can either take her back to Holly's gran's house and drop her off, or I can take her back to my place. If I give the choice to Banner, I know what she'll pick, but I'm not ready to let her go tonight. Even if she chooses not to sleep in my bed, I still have a strong need to see her in my space.

I turn right instead of left, and Banner, even in her buzzed condition, picks up on it.

"I thought my place was the other way. I know I came from that direction. I think."

She cranes her neck to look behind us, but in the darkness, there's not a single landmark for her to see. The county can't afford to keep this road lit up, so all the streetlights have been dark for years.

"We're going to my place."

She whips around to face me. "Why?"

"I want to show it to you."

She goes quiet. "What are we doing, Logan? We barely know each other. A couple weeks of texting and two one-night stands don't make us a couple."

My hands tighten on the steering wheel because her words are the truth, even if I don't want them to be.

"There's a reason you came running to Gold Haven, even if you won't admit it."

"It was a free place to stay," she says.

"There was a lot more to it than that, Banner, and we both know it." I look across the cab of the truck at her. "I'm pretty sure Greer would've put you up in New York for as long as you wanted. The fact that you chose to leave and walk into my world might not mean anything to you, but it means something to me. I could be reading into shit all wrong here, but there's something between us that's bigger than texts and one-night stands. Do you really think I needed to come to New York to deliver that car myself? No fucking way. But there's been something about you from the very beginning that called to me, and I had to follow my gut."

Her voice is quiet when she speaks again. "So, where do we go from here?"

I slow for a stop sign and meet her stare. "We're going to get to know each other. I'm going to take you out on dates and show you what we've both been missing. You're gonna fall in love with me, Banner. That's where we're going from here."

Her eyes widen again and go glassy for a moment before they break away.

I drive through the intersection and go straight toward my house.

"I've never fallen in love with anyone, so you've got your work cut out for you."

I let a smile stretch across my face. "I'm man enough for the job. There's no doubt in my mind about that."

Bringing Banner to my house has me looking at it through new eyes. It's not fancy, but I bought the place as a heap and turned it into a home I'm proud of. It's a long way from the rusted single wide I grew up in as a kid, and I know I'm lucky to have it.

I've seen Banner's apartment—or her former apartment—so I know she's used to more, but when we pull up in front of the cedar-sided house with a covered porch along the front and the motion light kicks on, she sucks in a breath.

"I love it."

Relief fills me at her declaration.

"You haven't even seen the inside." I turn off my truck

and hop out.

She doesn't wait for me to get her door, though, but meets me in front of the truck as she stares up at the house set back amongst a stand of trees. The gurgle of the creek running along the back corner of the yard breaks through the otherwise quiet night, even though the lights don't reach far enough for her to see it.

"Did you build it?"

I shake my head as I thread my fingers through hers and walk up to the front steps. "No, but I gutted it down to the studs and redid the entire inside. It was a foreclosure, and I picked it up cheap from the bank. It sits on five acres, so it's pretty private back here."

"Five acres?"

There's a certain amount of wonder in her voice, and I forget that she's a Manhattanite, and that kind of property is unheard of.

"Property's a lot cheaper in Kentucky than New York City."

We climb the stairs onto the porch and I push my key into the lock to take her in through the front door, flipping on the lights as we step inside. Normally, I'd come in through the back, but I wanted her to see the house this way instead.

I point up at the vaulted ceiling lined with tongue-and-groove pine. "That ceiling was a bitch to install by myself."

Her eyes widen. "You did that?"

I nod. "Every piece of this house has my blood, sweat, and cuss words wrapped up in it. The stacked-stone fireplace took forever to get right, but it was worth it. I'd come here after a long day at the shop and work until I was so tired, I couldn't trust myself with power tools."

Banner does a slow circle, taking in the room.

A gray couch and chair face the fireplace, and the TV hangs over the mantel. There's not much in the way of knickknacks because I've got a dick.

"I love it," she says again, and I swear I'm puffing up from the pride now. She hesitates before stepping on the re-finished pine floors, looking to me and down at her boots. "I don't want to track bowling alley nastiness all over your beautiful home."

"Your choice," I say.

She wobbles a little as she pulls her boots off, and suddenly she's three inches shorter.

I kick off my work boots as well, and lead her into the kitchen. It's open to the living room, and while it's not gourmet, it's pretty damn nice. "I picked out the remnant of granite myself, and traded out car repairs with a buddy to build the custom cabinets."

"I don't even know how to cook, but I'm definitely impressed."

"Luckily, we know I can cook, so you're not going to starve in the morning."

Before she replies, Banner zeroes in on the key rack by the back door. She walks over to it, reaching up to touch the Hulk key chain from the arcade in New York.

"You kept it." She turns to look at me, surprise in her eyes. "I figured you would've tossed it out the window as soon as you hit the highway. Especially after . . ." Her words trail off.

I shake my head and cross to where she stands. "I thought about it, but then I realized it didn't matter whether

I kept it or not. There was no way I'd ever forget you."

I don't mention the panties that are still in my toolbox. A man has to have some secrets.

Banner bites down on her lip and swallows. "I'm glad you kept it. It'd be sad if I were the only one carrying something around from that night." She digs in her purse and pulls out the keys to Holly's gran's house, and sure enough, there's the Wolverine key chain I won her.

"It was a good night."

She nods. "The best."

"Ah, Bruce." I give her a smile. "We can do better than that. Just wait."

My words hang between us, and even though I want to say more, I change the subject.

"You wanna see the rest?"

She nods, and I lead her up the hallway, showing her the second bathroom, a guest room, and a bedroom I turned into an office. Finally, I push open the door to the master. It's clear a man lives here by himself. There are only enough pillows on the bed to sleep, the comforter is a little rumpled where I tossed it over the sheets in an attempt to make the bed, and a pair of jeans and a T-shirt lie over a chair in the corner.

"So this is the famous bed of Logan Brantley."

I look at her sideways. "Famous? Not exactly."

"But half the women in this town want to say they've been in it."

"They haven't, and since I've got no plans to change that, they'll have to live with the disappointment." I nod toward the doorway across the room. "The master bath is through there. More showerheads than one man needs, but after I've been up to my elbows in grease and oil all day, I appreciate being clean."

Banner turns around to face me. "I really do love it. You did an incredible job, Logan."

Silence falls between us, and I find my plans for tonight aren't what I anticipated. As much as I want to spend the rest of the night inside Banner, right now what I want even more is to fall asleep with her in my arms in my own damned bed.

She's the game changer.

And now I've got my work cut out for me to make sure I win the game.

THIRTY-TWO

Banner

WHERE AM *I*?

I blink and take in the slate-blue-colored walls, and wood trim that looks nothing like anywhere I've ever been. The weight of an arm is wrapped around me, and heat presses against my back.

For a second, I wonder if I made a huge mistake, but then my mind kicks into gear.

Logan.

Logan's bed.

Logan's house.

And we didn't even have sex last night.

I have absolutely no idea how to navigate the waters, especially since he told me I'm going to fall in love with him. *I'm so out of my depth.*

"I swear I can feel your brain flipping on," Logan's deep voice rumbles in my ear. "Your whole body tenses like you're not sure whether you should bolt."

"It's creepy that you think you can read my mind," I whisper.

"Tell me I'm wrong."

"I'm thinking I have no idea how to handle this non-relationship of ours."

I find myself flat on my back, and Logan's big body hovering over me a moment later.

"This is a relationship, Banner. Have no doubt about that."

I wonder if my eyes bulge as big as they feel when he says it. "But—"

"No buts about it. We're dating. And we're going to have our first official Kentucky date tonight."

"We are? And why are you so bossy all of a sudden?"

"I've always been bossy. You just didn't mind because it was all in bed."

True story.

Logan lowers himself to his elbows, and his heavy erection presses into my thigh.

"I guess this qualifies because we're still in bed," I murmur.

His lips quirk into a smile. "We are, but unfortunately, I've got to get to work, which means we both have to get up so I can drop you off at your car so you're not stranded here all day."

"Shit. It's been at the bowling alley all night. Do you think someone stole it?" I ask, panic creeping in. A stolen rental car would not be cool, especially when it was rented for me as a favor.

Logan's smile turns playful. "This is Gold Haven. No one could steal a rental car and get away with it. It's fine." He leans down another three inches and brushes his lips over mine. "G'morning, Bruce."

"G'morning, Logan," I murmur as I return the kiss and chase his lips upward when they lift away. But I can't reach them for long because he heaves himself to the side and stands.

Clad in only boxer briefs, Logan's body is impressive. A light dusting of hair sprinkles over his pecs and trails down over his abs and navel to disappear under the waistband. *What is it about a man with a hard body? Why are my panties predisposed to drop?*

He winks before he turns and heads to the bathroom, and my greedy eyes are fixed on his ass. I don't know what he does to keep his body in that kind of shape, but I fully support it.

I haul my ass out of bed too. My cami and jeans both stink like bowling alley smoke, and I can't stomach the thought of putting them back on. I sniff the ends of my hair and grimace as I hear the shower turn on.

Maybe he wouldn't mind having some company. As many one-night stands as I've had, I've never done the couple-shower thing. Apparently there are still some areas where I'm a virgin.

I slip out of the T-shirt I borrowed last night without permission and head for the bathroom.

Logan is inside the glass-walled shower, soaping up when his eyes find mine. "You're more than welcome to join me."

I glance at the mirror and freeze before I take another step. "Holy Jesus, why didn't you tell me I looked like I belonged on *The Walking Dead*?"

My makeup is smudged beneath my eyes, giving me that near-death appearance, and my hair looks like it went one-on-one against the zombie apocalypse and lost.

Logan's laughter echoes in the glass enclosure. "And yet you're still sexy as hell. Get your ass in here."

"You have more showerheads in here than I did in mine."

"I doubt New York water pressure could handle more."

"Fair point."

My hair is soaked in moments, and I'm sure I now look like a drowned rat. "This isn't a shower, it's a freaking car wash," I say, turning away from the spray.

Logan hands me a bar of soap. "I don't have any girly shit for you to use, but I've got soap and shampoo and face wash, if you don't mind smelling like me. Well, me without the exhaust, brake fluid, grease, and oil."

He's mentioned that more than once, and I wonder if it bothers him. "If you could bottle how you smell when you step out of that garage after working for a day, you'd be a millionaire," I tell him with complete sincerity.

"Is that right?" Logan turns me to face him as he pushes my wet hair out of my face.

I nod.

"Then I'm glad you like it."

When our lips meet, I swallow his laughter.

His hands start on my shoulders, but they don't stay there. Logan's wide palms skim down my back until he's cupping my ass and sliding one hand between my cheeks.

I jump as his fingers brush over a particularly sensitive spot—also known as my asshole. I pull my head back and look at him. "You trying to give me the shocker?"

Logan's blue eyes are lazy when they meet mine. "The shocker?"

"When you slip two fingers in a girl's pussy and then shock her with one in the back door."

His fingertips trail over my asshole again, this time adding pressure. "Is that what you're hoping I'm going to do with this tight little ass?"

A moan escapes my lips as I rise up on my toes, not sure if I want to escape the pressure or push into it.

He follows my movements. "I'm not going to stop playing until you answer me."

"Maybe I'll never answer."

"Naughty little thing." Logan's touch falls away from my ass, but returns with a hand on each of my hips to spin me around to face the back of the shower. "Bend over."

"What?" I sputter, but he's already guiding my hands down to the inset bench in front of me.

"You're naked, that means you like when I take control, and I think I can spare a little time to dirty us both up before we get clean."

There's something about his words in that deep drawl that has wetness dripping between my legs, and I know it has nothing to do with the water spraying from the multiple showerheads.

"What do you mean?"

His hard shaft slides between the globes of my ass, and I freeze.

Oh my God, he's not going to . . .

"I'm gonna fit my cock inside that pretty ass of yours, but not yet. No, you're gonna have to be a really naughty fucking girl for me first."

Logan adjusts his position to press his cock between my legs, but his thumb hovers right over my asshole as he moves in and out, dragging through my wetness.

"How could I possibly be that naughty?" My teasing words come out on a ragged breath as my nipples tighten.

"Oh, I don't know . . . probably bending over and sticking that ass out, maybe reaching back and spreading your cheeks wide for me. Letting me eat that cunt and that ass until you're dripping. Then I might find some lube and see if I can fit a finger in that tight little hole. If you're really bad, I might have to spank you first."

Now I'm squirming in place, squeezing my thighs together, wishing he was doing everything he's saying.

I'm seconds away from reaching back and spreading my cheeks when the head of his cock nudges inside my pussy.

"But not right now. Right now, you get just the tip. You think we can get you off this way? My dirty fantasies making you so wet, you're ready to beg me to do whatever I want to you?"

I push back, wanting more, when his palm lands on the side of my right ass cheek.

"Bad girl. You're only going to get what I give you." He presses in an inch before retreating. "And nothing more."

I moan in frustration but he pushes in again, giving me a few more inches.

"Just the tip, Banner. Can you get yourself off with just the tip?" He bends down without giving me any more, but his fingers cover my clit. "Or do you need some help?"

Logan Brantley has some kind of voodoo magic wrapped up in those fingers, because he strums my clit like he's the master of it.

When my orgasm begins to break over me, he thrusts

inside the rest of the way. I scream, and it echoes as he pulls out before fucking into me over and over, never letting up the pressure on my clit.

I come again, my inner muscles clamping down on his cock so hard, I'm amazed he can pull it free. But when the hot sticky spurts of come land on my ass, followed by his hand, I know I'm so fucked.

This man owns my body, and there's nothing I can do about it.

THIRTY-THREE

Banner

I T TAKES ALL THE NONCHALANCE I CAN MUSTER TO WALK out of the bathroom and into the bedroom, acting like something potentially foundation-rocking didn't just happen.

Logan's casualness comes off much more naturally as he strides over to his dresser and grabs sweats and a long-sleeved shirt. "They might not be designer, but I figure they're better than putting those smoky ones back on."

I take the pile from him and pull them on. They're big enough to be laughable, but definitely better than the alternative.

He looks at the clock and curses. "Shit, I really gotta get moving." His eyes carry regret when he looks at me. "I don't mean to—"

"It's fine." My interruption is hurried. "Don't worry about it."

Logan studies me and I know he wants to say something else, but he doesn't.

"Next time, you're making me breakfast, though," I say,

holding my breath after I speak. I've officially made it clear that there's going to be a *next time*, and for me, that's about as much as I can handle right now.

"It's a deal."

Logan's smile is broad as we make our way out of the bedroom toward the front door. We both pause at the sight of my skinny-heeled boots on the mat.

"This might not be a fashion statement, but they're all I've got."

"I'll grab you a pair of socks and carry you to the car. You can drive home without shoes."

With that decided, Logan retreats to grab socks, and then proceeds to carry me to the car once I put them on.

From the vantage point of his very strong arms, and against his very hard chest—both of which I'm trying like hell to ignore so I don't cream all over his clean sweat-pants—the house is even cuter in the daytime than it was at night. Logan did a hell of a job with it.

Our ride to the bowling alley is quiet. I know I'm studiously avoiding analyzing what the hell just happened, and he seems to be doing the same. But strangely, the silence isn't awkward or heavy. It's . . . comfortable.

We reach the bowling alley a few minutes later to find only three cars in the parking lot, including my rental. Logan pulls up next to mine. A red car is a few spaces away, parked with its front end toward us.

"Is that guy asleep in the front seat?"

Logan is out of the truck and running toward the car before I can open my door. He bangs on the window and yells at the guy inside, but there's no movement that I can see from here.

"Jeff, open this fucking door. Wake the fuck up."

When there's still no response, Logan runs back to the truck, but bypasses the cab in favor of the bed. He's got some kind of bar in his hand, and I shrink back as he shatters the back window of the car.

Oh shit. This isn't good.

I grab my phone instinctively before I jump out of the truck. The sharp gravel stings the soles of my feet as I run toward Logan.

Somehow he already unlocked the driver's side door and has it open when he yells to me.

"Call 911! We need an ambulance right now."

Heart hammering and hand shaking, I do as he says, offering up the limited information I have to the operator. She keeps asking questions, but I answer most of them the same way—*I don't know.*

Logan pulls the man out of the car to lay on the ground before performing CPR like a seasoned pro.

"Any pulse?" I ask, because the operator keeps asking me.

Logan shakes his head, and I relay the information.

"They're on their way."

He continues compressions until I can tell he's tiring. I don't know what the hell I'm doing, but it can't be rocket science. I shove the phone in my pocket and drop to my knees on the ground beside him.

"My turn."

Logan nods, and I take over.

We switch back and forth for the longest minutes of my life. Sweat is dripping down both our faces, but I'm terrified it's a lost cause.

When the EMTs arrive, siren blaring, we move out of the way.

One EMT looks up at Logan as he checks for a pulse. "It's there. It's thready and easy to miss, but it's there. You might've just saved this guy's life."

Logan nods and steps away. "Good, because he used to be my stepbrother."

His admission echoes in my brain, and I struggle to comprehend it.

Logan comes back to where I'm standing in front of his truck, out of the way of the paramedics, and presses both hands to the hood beside me. His head drops forward as he sucks in long, deep breaths.

"Are you okay?" It's the dumbest question in the world, but I have no idea what else to say.

He lifts his head and looks at me. "I figured one day he'd turn up dead from an overdose. I just never figured I'd have a front-row seat to it."

I lay a hand on his shoulder. "You heard the EMT; you might've just saved his life."

"We, not me. And that's if he makes it. Not that he'd thank us for doing a damn thing."

It seems there's no love lost between Logan and his former stepbrother.

"I can follow you to the hospital and—"

Logan shakes his head. "I'm too fucking pissed to go anywhere near him right now. There's nothing I can say that Jeff would want to hear."

"Then we could—"

"I gotta call Jeff's uncle. Only family he's got left after his dad passed." Logan straightens. "If he pulls through, maybe Duane can finally get him into rehab. He's a pastor, so maybe he could pull some strings somewhere." Logan slams his hand against the metal hood, and I can feel his body shaking beside me. "Fucking Jeff," he murmurs.

"I'm so sorry."

"No, I'm sorry." He pushes off the hood and faces me. "Really fucking sorry this morning turned to shit." Logan's breathing evens out, but the lines around his eyes show the evidence of strain.

"It's not your fault. You jumped in there and did everything you could to save him. That's . . . amazing."

He leans in and presses his lips to mine. "I'm glad you think so, but anyone would've done the same thing. Now I gotta make some calls and get some people praying he'll pull through."

I touch my forehead to his. We're both sweaty, but I don't care. "You know what, Logan Brantley? You're a good man. He's lucky you were here. And you're wrong. Not just anyone would've done what you did."

"You were right there next to me, Bruce." He releases a long breath. "You gonna be okay? You want to come along with me?"

Logan's offer is sincere, but all my instincts say he needs some time alone to process what just happened.

"I should head home."

He pulls me against his chest and squeezes me tight for long moments before lifting me off my feet and carrying me to the rental car.

"I'm sorry, Banner."

"You've got nothing to be sorry for."

I click the remote to unlock it, and Logan pulls open

the door before lowering me inside.

"I'll grab your boots."

"Thank you."

I rest my head on the steering wheel as my entire body shakes with the aftermath of what just happened.

Life is short. Shorter for some than for others, so we have to make every moment count.

THIRTY-FOUR

Logan

FUCKING JEFF. WHAT I TOLD BANNER WAS THE truth—I always figured he'd end up OD'ing on whatever the fuck he poisoned himself with. If I had to guess now, I'd say meth.

I'm finally finishing up the last touches on the engine of the Mustang, thankfully with the help of both Jock and Rick today, because my head is not where it needs to be.

Rick turns down the music. "We got company." He jerks his chin toward the service door as one Officer Cody Reeves walks inside.

"You got a minute, Logan? I need to get a statement from you."

I've called the hospital twice to check on Jeff, and he's still hanging on, so I know Cody isn't here to notify me of his passing.

I pull my rag from my back pocket and tell Jock, "Finish this up, and then wipe it all down and make it goddamn shine."

"No problem, boss."

I head for the waiting room, and Cody follows me. There's still some coffee hanging out in the last pot that I brewed, so I pour us each a cup.

"It tastes like tar, but it can't be much different from what you're used to."

"Much appreciated." He takes the cup from my hand and grabs three packets of sugar out of the coffee can that holds all our extra shit for waiting customers.

"You here about Jeff?"

He nods. "Sure am."

"I don't have a lot to tell you."

"How about you start at the beginning."

"I pulled into the parking lot at Brews and saw his car. He looked like he was passed out in the driver's seat, and something about it struck me as off."

"What were you doing at Brews at eight o'clock this morning?"

The rest of the town probably already knew by now, and I was over worrying about gossip concerning me and Banner. "Bringing a woman back to her car."

"Banner Regent?"

I shoot him a hard look. "Why are you asking me questions you already know the answers to? Isn't this a waste of both our time?"

"It's procedure."

I look down at my coffee and take a breath. My patience is for shit today. "Yeah, Banner Regent. She spent last night at my house after we left Brews. I brought her back to get her car this morning so I could get to the shop early, but that didn't end up happening because my ex-stepbrother was in the process of OD'ing in the parking lot, and I had to give his rotted-ass meth mouth CPR so he didn't die." I meet Cody's gaze and see the sympathy there.

"How do you know he was OD'ing?"

"Educated guess."

"When's the last time you saw Jeff before this morning?"

Tipping my head back, I focus on a water spot on the ceiling tile above me. Absently, I remind myself to replace it because it looks like shit.

"The last time I saw him? Probably a few months ago in passing. I've seen his car around, but not him."

"What about the last time you talked to him?"

I look up at the ceiling again and think back. "A while."

"Exactly how long? And did you argue?"

I jerk my gaze back to Cody's. "Really? Is this important?"

"I wouldn't be asking the question if I didn't need an answer."

"Our parents were married for all of six months before his dad ended up in prison for possession while I was still in school, but you know all that. Jeff Senior caught a shank and bled out, and no one was sad to see him go."

"That's not what I asked."

"I told Jeff to go fuck himself the last time he came knocking. I'd just bought this place and was in a ton of debt, and he wanted money. He looked like shit, and I knew whatever I gave him would go straight to his dealer, so I told him if he ever stepped through my doorway again, I'd beat the hell out of him."

Cody nods like he finally has an explanation that satisfies him. "I wouldn't tell anyone else this, but I've known you way too fucking long not to. Jeff was dealing, and he was doing a shit job of keeping it on the DL, too busy using a ton of his own product. He's been under surveillance for weeks because we're trying to get a lock on exactly who he's buying from so we can bust the bigger fish. He's the bottom of the food chain, and we planned to take him down this week and get him to inform for us in exchange for a lesser sentence."

"So you're telling me I just helped save someone who's part of the problem in this town?"

Cody shrugs. "He's still unconscious, so we can't question him right now, but we have security stationed at his door just in case someone decides that he might be thinking about talking."

The implications of his words sink in. "You think Jeff's supplier is going to off him before he can talk?"

"It's a distinct possibility."

"Fucking hell. Can't you turn someone else?"

"We're trying."

"What a disaster."

Cody sucks back the rest of his coffee and tosses the cup in the trash. "I thought I'd come see if you had any idea who Jeff was close to these days, but I'm guessing from what you told me that's a no."

"You'd be right about that."

He turns and heads for the door. "I appreciate the coffee."

"If he wakes up, do you want me to talk to him? Try to get some answers?"

Cody pauses and glances back at me. "Nah, we got this covered. Thanks for the offer. And good luck with the woman. She seems a little different from the normal kind around here. Ain't looking to lock your ass down and throw away the key."

Cody was another guy in Gold Haven determined to stay single.

"She's definitely not that kind."

"I need to find me one of those," he replies before pushing the door open.

I want to tell him good luck, because women like Banner are one in a million and nothing like the kind he's used to, but I don't. I head back into the garage to find Jock and Rick have the music back on, and are shining up every surface under the hood for the Mustang we finished.

"Looking slick."

"Of course it does. This shop only does badass restorations."

I grunt in response, and my brain goes back through all the stuff Cody told me. Someone in this town is pushing meth, and my former stepbrother was dealing.

Fucking ridiculous.

THIRTY-FIVE

Banner

I CALLED THE HOSPITAL TO CHECK ON LOGAN'S EX-stepbrother, but they wouldn't even confirm if he was a patient. I know Logan promised to take me on a date tonight, but with the events of this morning, there's no way that's happening.

Instead, I knock out several hours of work before my stomach stages a rebellion. I could attempt to make something, but I decide to venture into town again and try the home-style family restaurant I saw when I was semi-stalking Logan last night. It was closed then, so I figure it caters to more of the early-bird-special clientele.

After I take a half hour to make myself look presentable—well, more like make it so the women in town won't be able to find anything bad to say about my appearance if they tried—I take my rental car into town and park in front of Home Cookin'.

When I step inside the glass door, there's a white piece of notebook paper on a podium to write your name and the number in your party. I've missed the lunch crowd, so there's no one in the waiting area and no names left open on the list. Green vinyl booths line both side walls, and there are several empty tables mixed in with the few taken up by older folks drinking coffee. An honest-to-God lunch counter with stools runs along the back section of the restaurant.

A woman in jeans, cowboy boots, and a green polo shirt with *Home Cookin'* embroidered on the breast comes toward me.

"How many in your party?"

"Just one, thanks."

"Do you want a seat at the counter, or would you like a table or booth?"

"A booth would be great."

She pulls a plastic menu, a paper place mat, and napkin-wrapped silverware out of the three wooden holders on the paneled half wall next to the waiting-list stand. "Follow me right this way."

I trail after her, impressed by the way her Levi's hug her curves without causing the dreaded muffin top. I have to spend big dollars on jeans to ensure the same effect.

"You can have a seat right here. Great view of the main drag through town, so you can do some people watching."

It also has a great view of Logan's repair shop, such that I can see his truck parked around the side.

"Thanks, this is perfect." I look up at her name tag. "I appreciate it, Emmy."

"Can I get you something to drink?"

"A skinny caramel latte would be great."

Her eyebrows wing up to her hairline. "I'm afraid that's a forty-five-minute drive. In this town, you've got coffee and hot chocolate, unless you want one of those instant cappuccino drinks out of the machine at the gas station, but I hear that's all sugar and chemicals."

"Do you have Diet Coke?"

She nods. "Of course."

As she walks off, I can hear her mutter, "Skinny caramel latte . . . where does that girl think she is?"

I study the menu, deciding to skip the chicken fried steak because I have absolutely no idea what the hell it is, and instead choose a Caesar salad with chicken.

A different woman comes to the table with my Diet Coke and to take my order. Her name tag says Darlene, and she's all business with her curly short dark brown hair.

"Dressing on the side?" she asks, beating me to my last request.

"Yes, please." I pause. "How did you know?"

She gives me a slow once-over. "You look like the type." Darlene turns on a heel and heads back to put in my order.

I brush off her comment and stare out the window as what seems like a parade of trucks pass by. *Does every man in this town own a pickup truck? And when did that become so sexy?*

I'm sure there's only one answer for that, and it's all Logan Brantley's fault.

Emmy's voice cuts through the quiet chatter in the room. "I said I wanted his lunch ready in ten minutes. Do you want the man to starve?"

The door chimes again, and a woman with a killer fishtail braid strides in and up to the counter with the biggest travel mug I've ever seen. It must fit a half gallon of whatever she puts in it.

"Can I get a large coffee to go?"

Emmy turns around and eyes her. "That stuff is going to kill you someday, Julianne. You should really lay off the caffeine."

"Save the concern for someone who cares, Emmy." She twists the lid off the mug, and Emmy takes it from her before turning away to fill it up with an entire carafe of coffee.

Julianne, a woman I haven't yet met, slides some money across the counter and replaces the lid.

"You ever going to replace that broken coffeepot of yours?" Emmy asks, picking up the money and tucking it in the cash register. "Not that I'm complaining about taking your money."

"Warranty replacement is supposed to be here next week. Don't worry; I'm ready to end these lovely visits too."

Julianne turns away from the counter and heads for the door, but slows and changes direction when she notices me. "Well, well . . . I'm guessing I know exactly who you are."

"That's a little creepy." I didn't mean to say it out loud, but apparently my lack of filter is still well and truly intact.

She steps toward the table and sets down the giant travel mug. "I'm Julianne. I cut your man's hair, and you've got the entire town talking today." She slides into the booth without an invitation.

"Uh, feel free to join me, I guess."

"Thanks for the invite, but I've only got ten minutes before my next appointment, and I definitely am gonna have to pee." She stares at me as she sucks down a sip of coffee. "Do you know how many women in this town probably wouldn't mind accidentally hittin' you with a car today after hearing about what Logan said last night at Brews and

Balls?"

"I expected this conversation to get less creepy, but it turns out I was wrong."

Julianne shrugs. "I'm just saying you might want to watch your ass. He's a catch, and he's been evading the net for a while now. Some of these women are getting desperate." She shoots a look toward Emmy behind the counter as the other woman tucks some food into what looks like a picnic basket. "That one, especially."

"Her? Really?" My next inspection of Emmy is much closer. Acceptably cut light brown hair, decent body, nice eyes, and a hint of bitchiness.

Julianne nods when I meet her gaze again. "She's carved her name in his tree, if you know what I mean."

I might not be from Kentucky, but even I understand her euphemism. "I get what you're saying."

"But apparently Emmy hasn't put two and two together that you're the one who's about to crush her dreams of becoming Mrs. Logan Brantley."

When she glances back at the woman, I follow her gaze. "Why's that?"

"She'd be glaring daggers at you instead of putting Logan's lunch basket together."

Logan's lunch basket? Seriously? "Did he order takeout?"

Julianne laughs. "Nope. He doesn't have to in order to get the Emmy special. She makes it her mission to keep him fed. I guess she's trying to get the one half of the *stomach full, balls empty* equation covered, since as far as I know, Logan's never let her get anywhere near his balls." Julianne sips her coffee again. "Not for lack of trying, of course. She'd for sure turn up pregnant the first time he touched her, though. I'd put money on that."

All of this information is bringing on an epically bad headache and killing my appetite.

I narrow my eyes at Julianne. "Why are you telling me this?"

She shrugs. "Logan genuinely likes you. He's made that plenty clear." She shoots a look over at Emmy. "And I've pretty much hated that bitch since junior high when she decided she was better than everyone else."

God bless small towns.

A short bus pulls up in front of the restaurant, momentarily blocking my view of the street.

"I better get out of here. The assisted-living-home folks are coming for their *way too late to be* lunch and *too early to be* dinner. It's about to be old people city up in here. See you around, Banner. You let me know if you need that color touched up or those nails fixed. I'm not a big-city stylist by any means, but I don't fuck up hair or nails." She flashes me a crooked smile. "Just everything else in my life."

And with that, she's gone, leaving me wishing she'd stayed longer. Besides Nicole, Julianne is the only other woman I've met in this town I can picture having drinks with.

Emmy bustles to the door as the busload of older people comes tromping into the restaurant. "Y'all are early! I didn't expect you until three thirty."

Darlene rushes over with my salad and drops it at the table. "You need anything else? I'm about to be real busy."

"No, ma'am. I'm all set here."

I lean back in the booth and proceed to be entertained by all the retirees and their chatter. There's some kind of magic to this small-town life.

———————✦———————

Julianne's warning about Emmy and her plans concerning Logan keep cycling through my head as I finish my salad. It wasn't incredibly filling, but I didn't have to make it myself, so there's that. The door to the restaurant chimes again, and I realize this place must be a happening spot in town for all the traffic I've seen.

"I thought that was your rental out front. How's it going, Bruce?"

Logan slides into the booth the same way Julianne did. Every time he calls me Bruce, a shaft of warmth hits me directly in the heart-attack region.

Apparently I'm not the only one who notices Logan, though. Emmy comes right over to my table.

"I'm so sorry, Logan. I had a late lunch all packed up for you but the Sunnybrook contingent distracted me." She looks from Logan to me and then back at him. "You don't have to share a booth with her; we've got plenty of open tables."

Awkwardness fills the void as soon as she shuts her mouth.

Logan smiles at me before he speaks. "This is exactly where I want to be sitting." He finally glances up at Emmy. "Have you met Banner? She's in town from New York."

As soon as he says my name, the confused expression on her face turns into something harsh before immediately morphing into the fakest smile I've ever seen. And considering I'm from New York, that's saying something.

"I didn't get her name. Welcome to our little slice of

paradise, ma'am. I'm sure you're already bored out of your mind, what with you being from the big city and all."

"I'm just getting settled in, and I can't imagine leaving anytime soon." My tone carries a sincerity that Logan can't miss.

The edges of Emmy's fake smile start to roughen. "Oh, I'm sure you'll be done with this place soon enough."

Logan's watching our exchange, and he's not an idiot. "I sure hope not. I appreciate you making Banner feel welcome. She's pretty damn special to me."

Emmy's mask threatens to crack, but she holds it in place. "*Special.* How sweet. I'll just leave you two alone then. Unless you still want the club sandwich and blueberry pie I packed up for you. It's on the house, as always."

I wait to see how Logan will respond.

"I gotta get back to work in a few. I only had a minute to run over here because I saw Banner's car. You know you don't need to keep bringing me lunch. I can handle myself."

"Well then," Emmy says, her teeth clenched. "I'll just leave you alone."

She steps away and nearly runs smack into Darlene, who is carrying a tray of refills to a table.

"That was . . . interesting," I say, looking at Logan after Emmy stalks away.

"We went out a few times, but we were really never more than friends," he says in explanation.

I haven't decided if I feel threatened or not. I decide *not* because according to Julianne's gossip, Emmy doesn't even know about the good dick she's missing out on.

"She wanted to be a whole lot more, though, I bet."

Logan covers my hand with his. "Doesn't matter,

because there's gotta be two people who want the same thing in order for something like that to happen."

It's on the tip of my tongue to ask why he didn't want anything to happen with Betty Crocker Barbie, but I decide that now isn't the time or place.

"You don't have to turn down her food on my account." Although, for some stupid, petty reason, I'm hoping he sticks to his decision.

"I've got a couple protein bars that'll tide me over. But that's not what I came to talk to you about."

I take in his stiffening posture. "What's wrong?"

"Nothing. Well, that's not true. It's been a shit day, and I know I said I wanted to take you out on a date, but I'm gonna go up to the hospital tonight to see what I can find out, and that's not where I want to take you. Do you mind if we make it a rain check?"

Even though I'm disappointed by the idea of not seeing Logan tonight, I completely understand where he's coming from.

"Of course I don't mind."

Logan relaxes in the booth. "Thanks, Bruce. This isn't something I saw coming."

I reach out and cover his hand with mine. It's not a gesture that's normal for me, but with Logan, it feels exactly right. "You do what you need to do. Don't worry about me. I've got enough work to keep me busy for two weeks."

He threads his fingers through mine and squeezes. "Thanks, Bruce."

When I move to pull my hand back, he stops me. "You ever going to tell me exactly what that work is?"

The edges of my lips turn up with a smile as I think

about all the retirees in the room. "Now really isn't the time or place. But when you cash in on that rain check . . . I'll tell you."

Surprisingly, I'm excited about the prospect of telling Logan.

"It's a deal. And I promise I'll make tonight up to you," he says as he finally releases my hand and stands.

Before I can reply, Logan leans down and presses a kiss to my lips, and I think the entire restaurant freezes at the same moment I do.

Holy crap. Logan's not messing around with this.

"I'll talk to you later, Bruce."

I nod, feeling the weight of all the stares in the room. Logan turns and takes a few steps before pausing.

"You wanna toss those steaks I left at your place in the freezer? We can grill 'em up next time."

The weight of the stares intensifies.

"That sounds perfect," I say, keeping my smile intact.

"Catch you later."

The chime rings as Logan strides out of the restaurant, but all the patrons inside seem to be content continuing to stare at me, including Emmy. But where the rest of them seem curious, she looks enraged.

I push my empty plate away and pull a twenty from my wallet to leave on the table rather than waiting for my bill.

It appears I've overstayed my welcome at Home Cookin'.

THIRTY-SIX

Logan

I T FEELS GOOD STAKING MY CLAIM ON BANNER. I'VE never before had the compulsion to do something like that, but with her, it's exactly what I want. Gossip is going to happen either way, and she's proven she's tough enough to handle whatever comes her way.

I've been busting my ass to put the final touches on this Mustang all day, and when the owner shows up and takes a look at his fully restored car and his eyes go glassy, I know I've done my job right.

The classic restorations take a lot more labor, but the big fat paychecks make them worth it. Oil changes and routine repairs are my bread and butter, but restorations are what I truly enjoy.

"You guys can call it a night," I tell Jock and Rick at six thirty. "I'm just waiting for our next project to get dropped off, and that doesn't take all of us sitting around."

Both men nod and head for the sinks to scrub away the grease and grime they've accumulated through the day.

Rick disappears quickly, but Jock stops before he heads

out. "You hear any word on Jeff?"

I shake my head. "Hospital says there's no change yet."

"So he could go either way?"

"That's what they're saying. I'm heading up there tonight to get more answers."

"It's a shame he got caught up in that shit. My cousin's kid got picked up with some ice. I swear, it's a fucking epidemic."

"It sure seems that way, doesn't it?"

"Between you and me, there's a guy in my pool league who all of a sudden is driving a new truck and flashing a lot of cash. I think he's dealing, but I'm not about to narc on him."

And that's the problem with drugs in a small town. Ninety percent of people aren't going to get involved, even if they know something's not right. But then again, that's how the gossip and finger-pointing actually stay at a minimum.

"You got any idea who's supplying it to him?"

Jock shakes his head. "Nope. Not a clue, but he's barely trying to hide it now. I'm hoping he figures his shit out and gets clear of it before something like this happens to him. He's got two kids, man."

I wonder silently if that's how Jock's buddy justifies what he's doing—making money to give his kids a better life than he had. Around here, there's not much opportunity for jobs that pay well, aside from the furniture factory and the hospital.

"I hope he gets clear of it too."

Jock nods and heads out the door while I wash up.

A half hour later, a jacked-up black Chevy truck pulls in with a rusted-out 1969 Oldsmobile 442 on a flatbed trailer. The man who climbs out of the passenger seat is one I've only ever seen on TV, and I head outside to meet him.

"Sorry I'm late. Got caught in some traffic outside of Nashville. Who knew Bumfuck, Kentucky, was so goddamned far away." His voice sounds just as gravelly as it does when he's onstage.

"Shit. When I saw 'B. Thrasher' on the work order, I didn't expect to see Boone Thrasher rolling up here."

The country singer holds out a hand. "We've got a mutual friend, and she says you're the guy to fix up this rusted-out wreck for me."

Holly Wix is the only person he could possibly be talking about. Seems she's sending a lot of interesting things into my life lately.

"Oh, she did, did she?"

"So don't make a liar out of Holly, because I'll be holding it against her and not you."

I can tell by his tone that he's joking . . . sort of.

"I don't think we'll have a problem. Let's go inside, and I'll grab a sketch pad. This is the kind of project I need to draw."

"I like you already," Thrasher says, following me inside.

We spend the next hour talking about his options as I sketch out a rough idea of the design. Black and red. Classic interior, but details unique to Boone, like brass knuckles and skulls. We both stare down at the pad when I finish.

"It's going to be slick as shit when it's done," I tell him. "You've got good taste, man."

Thrasher shrugs. "I got more money than taste, but I'm counting on you not to let it look like shit. You've got the reputation to uphold, and if it comes out like I'm thinking, you're going to have a hell of a lot of business coming your way. I'll get this beast into every classic-car mag out there, and then people will be bustin' down your door."

If Boone Thrasher is true to his word, my business will be changed forever. Not just pushed to the next level, but into the stratosphere. I shove down my excitement because I've gotta prove myself first and see what happens.

"Then I better make sure you're in love with this car when it's done."

"Fucking right."

"You turning around and driving back to Nashville tonight?" I ask as he crosses his arms over his chest and nods.

"Yes, sir. I've got a tour kicking off in a couple days, and they get pretty pissed if I'm not on that bus when I need to be."

I can only imagine what his life must be like.

"I'm kinda surprised you drove all the way out here yourself."

He gives me a shrug. "This isn't the kind of project I can pawn off on a roadie or an assistant. I needed you to hear from me exactly what I wanted."

"Understood. I'm not going to let you down, man."

"Good. How long you think it'll take?"

"Give me eight weeks, just because I don't know how long it's going to take to get all the body pieces replaced, and I'll see what I can do."

Thrasher looks at the car. "I'm on the road for six, and I really want it waiting for me at my last show in Nashville. I've been writing this new song that goes to the heart of everything I am, and the whole time we've been talking, I've been picturing driving the car out onstage to debut my new single. You think you could make that happen? I promise I'll make it worth your while. Press, photo shoot, everything."

Shit, with that kind of incentive . . .

"I can make it happen."

"Much appreciated, sir. Now, let's get this beast off my trailer and into your shop."

THIRTY-SEVEN

Banner

MY PHONE DINGS FROM THE COUNTER AS I SHUT MY laptop in my makeshift office—aka the kitchen. I reach behind me to grab it, stretching my neck from side to side.

How long have I been sitting here? A glance at the clock tells me it's been hours. The ache disappears the moment I look down at the screen of my phone and see a text from Logan.

> LOGAN REAL MAN BRANTLEY: *I'm finally cashing in that rain check. Sorry it took me so long.*

He's telling the truth on that score. Logan has been working his ass off on a new restoration project that he's crazy excited about, and I've been working night and day troubleshooting yet another design issue. Given our intense focus on our respective projects, we've reverted to texts as our primary means of conversation for the last seven days.

Maybe other women would be annoyed, but I've been

too busy to worry about it.

With a smile on my face, I tap out my reply.

> BANNER: *Don't apologize. I've been busy too. Just tell me when and where.*
> LOGAN REAL MAN BRANTLEY: *My place. 8 p.m. I'll grill those steaks from your freezer. Work for you?*
> BANNER: *I'll be there. Can't wait.*
> LOGAN REAL MAN BRANTLEY: *Good. I miss you, Bruce. It's been too long since I've seen my girl.*

A shiver of something I can't quite name travels down my spine at the words *my girl*. Even in his texts, Logan isn't shy about making it clear where he stands.

Nervousness starts to creep in about tonight. Like it's going to be some big step in the relationship he says we're in.

I still haven't gotten around to admitting to myself that I jumped at the chance to come to Gold Haven because I wasn't ready for this fascination I had with him to be over. *Or maybe I just did.*

> BANNER: *I agree.*

I pull up to Logan's house at eight, thawed steaks from my freezer in a bag on the passenger seat, along with two giant potatoes and a bag of premade salad I picked up. Piggly Wiggly isn't as treacherous now that I'm a seasoned pro at small-town grocery-store encounters.

When I knock on the front door, there's a thirty-second

delay before Logan pulls it open.

My mouth goes dry. His dark hair is wet, and a water droplet slides from his shoulder over his pec and down the line between his abs until it soaks into the towel at his waist.

That's not the only thing that's soaking.

"My eyes are up here."

When I finally drag my gaze back up to his face, a smile tugs at the corners of his mouth.

"I know. But you're wet."

"I am."

"What a coincidence. So am I."

Logan's grin widens. "Is that right?"

I nod. A week is way too long to go without getting naked with him.

"Then you should probably get in here instead of standing outside all night."

"Okay." I step over the threshold, and the scent of clean *man* hangs in the air as Logan reaches around me to close the door.

"Sorry, I got caught up working on the 442—"

I drop the bags to the floor, and my hands land on his pecs before I lean up to cover his lips with mine. Logan doesn't miss a beat as his arms close around me, and both hands find my ass to lift me up. Apparently, he missed me just as much.

My skirt, the one I picked out especially for tonight, slides up my thighs as I wrap my legs around him.

Nothing has ever turned me on as much as the sight of Logan Brantley dripping wet in a towel.

His hands slip under my skirt as he presses my back against the door. He tears his lips away from mine. "Fuck, you're not wearing any panties."

I shake my head.

"Jesus, woman. I was going to wait until after dinner, eat your pussy for dessert and then fuck you in front of the fire, but—"

"Now's better," I say, interrupting him. "We can do all that later."

I reach down and shove the towel off his hips. As soon as my fingers wrap around his cock, Logan lets out a groan.

"Fuck . . ."

"Yes, that. Let's do that."

He presses me harder against the door as the head of his cock finds my entrance. "Are you on the pill? I didn't ask before."

I shake my head. "The shot. And I'm clean."

"You want my cock?"

"Hurry."

"Answer me, Banner."

"Yes!"

"You're gonna take it every way I wanna give it to you tonight?"

My inner muscles clench at his words. "Yes."

"That's right. You're my naughty fucking girl."

"*Please*."

He buries his cock inside me in one thrust and I throw my head back, not caring that it connects with the door.

"Careful, baby." One of Logan's hands releases my ass and cups the back of my head. "Careful."

"I'm okay."

"Hold on tight."

I wrap both arms around his shoulders and grip the

solid muscles as he starts to move. With every deep thrust, my clit rubs against him and my orgasm rises. He never slows, just fucks into me over and over until I'm thankful his hand is blocking my head from slamming into the door, because I can't control my movements.

Suddenly, Logan steps back and carries me to the couch, laying me over the arm and arching my spine. He grips my hips with one hand as he presses down hard on my clit with his other thumb, and he varies his speed from fast strokes to long, slow ones. It's my undoing.

His name is on my lips as my fingernails dig into the couch cushions, and my climax shreds my control.

But Logan isn't satisfied. "Again."

I'm liquid. Boneless. I'm not even sure I can speak, but my body is on board with his command. I'm not sure if the first orgasm continues or if there's a second one, but I'm arching against it as his face twists with pleasure.

I close my eyes, trying to gather myself as my lungs heave for breath.

Holy. Shit.

Logan leans forward and presses a kiss between my breasts. "Next time, I'm going to play with these nipples until you're begging for me."

A laugh escapes from my lips.

After we've cleaned up and I shimmy my rucked-up skirt back down around my hips, I turn to Logan, who's now wearing a worn pair of jeans and nothing else.

"I'm pretty sure you can't top that appetizer."

THIRTY-EIGHT

Logan

BANNER TRIED TO TAME HER HAIR, BUT I LIKE THE *JUST been fucked by Logan Brantley* look on her. No woman has ever made me lose control the way she does. I felt it in New York, and I feel it here. Eventually, I'm going to get a handle on myself, but part of me doesn't want that to happen anytime soon.

She looks good in my house too, even if all she's doing is stabbing potatoes with a fork to pop in the microwave, or shaking some shredded lettuce into a bowl. The rest of my life might be chaos, but there's something about Banner that makes me forget about all of it.

I'm probably fucked, and I don't care.

After I pull the steaks off the grill and the potatoes are on our plates with the salad, we take seats at my bar because I still don't have a kitchen table.

One thing has been nagging at me all week, though, and she promised me an answer tonight.

"You're finally going to tell me what you're working on."

Banner almost chokes on a piece of steak before

washing it down with half a glass of water. "That came out of nowhere."

"I'm cashing in the whole rain check. You promised me an explanation tonight, and I gotta know. I've been driving myself crazy trying to figure it out."

She sets her water down and meets my gaze. "You really want to know that bad?"

"As long as you're not selling drugs," I start, but then cut myself off. That hits too close to home right now to be funny, considering Jeff is still in the hospital and by no means in good shape.

Banner shakes her head. "Definitely not drugs."

I wait for another minute before she finally tells me.

"I have patents pending on two new vibrators, and I'm going to sell sex toys."

I lower my fork to my plate as a smile stretches my lips. "Is that right? And you, the bluntest person I've ever met, don't want to tell people this . . . why?"

She bites her lip. "I don't think anyone will take me seriously. I can't exactly explain that I did my market research all by myself, and narrowed it down to what I believe are the two best and most efficient ways to get yourself off. And then I created two new vibrator designs that are basically idiot-proof so more women can finally have regular orgasms."

Her passion comes through loud and clear, and it's a good look on her.

"You haven't told anyone?"

"Two lawyers, a freelance engineer, the factory that created the prototypes and is getting ready for the first full run, and a marketing firm."

"You've got some coming here?"

She nods. "Yep. A box of dicks, if you will. Actually, that's how I got fired."

"What do you mean?"

"I screwed up and had my prototypes sent to my office. The boxes got piled up outside my cube, and a coworker of mine decided she had to know what was in them, so she opened one. Apparently she wasn't used to being wrist-deep in dicks because she freaked and dropped one on the floor, which of course turned on and vibrated its way just far enough into the hall for a senior VP to trip on. He landed face-first on the floor, broke a wrist *and* chipped a tooth, and I had to explain that my dick was the culprit."

I'm holding my sides laughing by the time she finishes the ridiculous story. "You're fuckin' with me. You have to be."

Banner shakes her head, a smile tugging at the corner of her mouth. "I'm really not. I couldn't make this shit up if I tried."

"Jesus Christ. You don't do anything halfway, do you, Bruce? So, when is this box of dicks coming to Gold Haven? Do I need to warn the post office?"

"In a couple weeks, if everything works out the way it should with production. And you better not warn them. I'm not taking the blame for any heart attacks over this."

"All right, deal. No warning. But I gotta say, it's hard to be sad you got fired, because this is all really fucking cool, Banner. I'm proud of you."

Her smile wobbles. "You're probably the only one, because I can guarantee my parents won't be anything but humiliated when they find out."

"So screw them. If they can't handle the fact that their daughter is talented in her own way, then they don't deserve to share in it."

The wobble disappears from her smile. "And here I figured you'd offer to help me test them out."

"You don't have to ask me twice about that. But I mean it, Banner. This is really fucking cool, and you should be proud."

"I'll be proud when I get the products and they work. I'm already working out teaser marketing campaigns, and I hope to God it all comes together. I've sunk so much into this that if it doesn't work out, I'm going to be broke for a while."

There's no doubt in my mind the incredible woman in front of me can accomplish anything she puts her mind to. "It's going to work. I have faith in you."

"Thank you. That means a lot. You probably didn't realize that I was a little jealous of the fact that you're a successful business owner, and I'm just sitting over here with a fake dick and a dream."

My laughter echoes off the vaulted ceilings of the house. When I finally can catch my breath, I tell her the thought that's been playing on a loop in my head all night. "I like having you here."

She lowers her water glass to the bar. "I like being here."

"Then it's a good thing I'm not planning on letting you leave for a while, isn't it?"

Her eyebrows go up. "You did make some promises about my pussy being on the menu for dessert, and something about fucking in front of a fire?"

"I'm glad you didn't forget. I fully intend to keep my promises."

She pushes her plate away. "I think I'm finished."

"Oh, hell no. You finish that steak. You're going to need your energy, babe."

THIRTY-NINE

Banner

WHEN ONE-NIGHTERS ARE YOUR GIG, THERE'S no chance of falling into any kind of a routine with someone. But Logan Brantley and Gold Haven are changing all of that for me.

It's been a week and a half since I last stepped foot in Manhattan, and although I miss the convenience of being able to get Ethiopian, Brazilian, and Hungarian food within a six-block radius, I've learned about the deliciousness of Mr. Burger seasoned fries, free homemade fudge tastings at the gift-shop counter in the pharmacy, and the fact that watching Logan grill a steak is on the list of *sexiest things to watch men do,* falling somewhere below meeting his eyes in the mirror as he pounds into me, and the way his head looks between my legs while he's making me scream.

Basically, I'm one endorphin-happy girl who is having mind-blowing sex with an amazing man, and I'm starting to think my stance on relationships could never have been changed by anyone but this man.

In other words, I'm fucked.

I really like this guy.

Like, *really* like him.

Maybe even more than like him.

I've only halfway felt the word that rhymes with *glove* once in my life, and it didn't end well. Now, sitting at the bar in Logan's kitchen as we finish our dinner, I'm having a bit of an internal crisis.

I don't know how to tell him. I don't even know if I *should* tell him. I don't doubt that he likes having me around, but little things tell me he still hasn't lost his wariness of women trying to tie him down as a paycheck.

And here I am with no income still as I work out my design issues so I can get my business fully off the ground.

I make the executive decision: I'm not going to say it first. It might not be the mature decision, but it's the only one that works for me.

I don't know if I could handle him telling me that he just doesn't feel that way, or telling me it's time to move on now that I've gotten attached. After all, I'm the girl you screw around with, not the one you settle down with.

When the hell did I start thinking in terms of settling down?

Logan pushes his plate away, but I still have half a steak and a salad to finish.

I'm not sure if I'm scared that I'm going to blurt something out, but right now I don't trust myself enough not to start babbling because I'm having a minor meltdown.

I'm twenty-seven. I'm the CEO of a broke company that no one has ever heard of—but I'm planning to make it a household name in the orgasm-delivery business. Settling down shouldn't even be in my plans right now.

"Something wrong with the steak, Bruce?" Logan asks.

I shake my head and cut another piece to pop into my mouth, industriously chewing like my life depends on it.

"So, I was thinking," he says, "dinner isn't enough of a rain check. Maybe we should get away for a weekend together. I know this place up in the Smokies that people sometimes use for honeymoons, but—"

I choke on the meat and start coughing.

"Jesus, are you okay?"

My eyes are watering, and I sound like I'm about to hack up a lung. I reach for my water and chug some to dislodge the meat.

"Do you need the Heimlich?" Logan stands up, poised to wrap his arms around my chest and start the maneuver.

I shake my head, reaching for my napkin to cover my mouth as I spit out the chunk and crush it into a ball.

"I'm okay." My voice comes out as a wheeze, and Logan stares at me like I've grown a third eye.

"Are you sure?"

I nod, reaching for my water again to calm my angry throat. "Just went down wrong."

I still sound like I've been strangled, but it's the best I can do as I reach over the edge of the counter for a piece of paper towel to wipe at the tears still leaking from the corners of my eyes.

He studies me for a moment before sitting back down. "Too much with the weekend thing?"

I shake my head. "Just bad timing with me trying to stuff my face."

"So I should wait to ask you until I'm balls deep and keep you on the edge of orgasm until you say yes?"

My Logan-loving lady parts perk up at that question.

"I can tell you like that idea," he adds.

"I guess you'll have to try it and see," I reply, hoping it comes off casually, even though I feel like there's a flashing neon sign above my head that says NONE OF THIS IS CASUAL ANYMORE.

"I think that's exactly what I should do. Who knows what I could get you to say if I started withholding orgasms."

He'd probably have me screaming out "I love you" in minutes. I freeze. *Holy. Shit.*

Desperate to change the subject to something less terrifying, I blurt, "Maybe we should try anal."

This time Logan's the one choking on a sip of beer.

"Are you okay?"

He nods and coughs a few more times before setting the glass down. "Not that I have a problem with it, but where the hell did that come from?"

I reach for my water and take a sip. "It's not like we haven't been dancing around it. And I thought the answer to anal was always a yes without question or hesitation."

Logan's gaze collides with mine. "The answer to sliding into that tight little ass of yours isn't just a yes, Banner. It's a *fuck yes*." Despite the heat in his blue eyes, he's still studying me as if he's trying to read between the lines to figure out what prompted my awkward-as-hell subject change.

"That's a relief because if you weren't interested, that would be a great sign that you're ready to move on."

When Logan raises an eyebrow, I realize I've tipped my hand.

"Is that what you're worried about? That I'm gonna lose interest?"

This time, I'm not the least bit subtle about shoving a forkful of salad into my mouth to prevent me from answering, and he connects the dots.

Logan leans back in his stool and crosses his arms over his broad chest.

"Are you serious? You're the one who's worrying *I'm* gonna lose interest, when I've got to compete with the entire borough of Manhattan to keep you here, and I've only got my cock and some seasoned fries from Mr. Burger as motivation."

I lean across the counter. "Your cock is a pretty powerful motivator, though."

"But what if it isn't enough?"

I swallow back a little of the fear and meet his stare. "No pun intended, Logan, but you're the whole package."

"So are you, Bruce. So are you."

My heart fills so full, I feel like it might explode. This moment is big, so of course I have to screw it up because I'm terrified of what I might say next.

"That's a yes to anal tonight?"

FORTY

Logan

I PARK IN THE CLOSEST NON-HANDICAPPED SPOT TO THE door of the CVS three towns over because neither Piggly Wiggly nor I have the right kind of lube, and the pharmacy is already closed for the night. This is the only twenty-four-hour place within fifty miles.

We both hop out of my truck, even though I'm sure Banner can do this without me. Still, I'm a gentleman, and I'm not going to make her buy the lube. I meet her on the sidewalk and slide my hand into hers.

She squeezes my fingers. "Do you feel naughty? I haven't felt naughty about buying lube since I was . . . never mind how old I was, but it's been a long time. Why is this different?"

"Probably because if we see anyone we know, the entire town is going to find out that I'm the luckiest man around." I pause. "Actually, they already know that, but this would confirm it."

Banner rolls her eyes at me. "Like we're going to see anyone I know. Maybe you, but not me."

"You know almost as many people as I do at this point. When the population is just over two thousand, it doesn't take long. Besides, you're the one who felt the need to be social when we were at Brews."

She doesn't reply but pulls me along behind her into the store and heads toward the back. I'm scanning faces as we walk. Banner stops at the end of an aisle and reaches out to grab a box. Then she puts it back and grabs a bigger box before looking up at me with a grin.

"We might as well supersize it."

Shuffling footsteps come from behind us, and I glance over my shoulder to see Mrs. Harris, Emmy's mom, coming down the vitamin aisle, still dressed in her housecoat and curlers.

Fuck.

I drag Banner around the corner by a hand, and her eyes dart up to mine and then behind me.

"Who's that?" she whispers.

"Emmy Harris's mom."

I can hear the woman's trademark humming as it grows louder. We edge closer to the pharmacy area, where I see another familiar face.

Nicole is standing at the counter, and the pharmacy tech tells her, "I'm sorry, ma'am, but I can't sell you any pseudoephedrine products right now."

Banner catches my eye, and we both hurry toward the other side of the store and dart up the aisle. In our hurry, Banner reaches out and grabs a bag of Doritos and shoves it into my arms.

"Quick. Get in line. I'm getting ice cream, and I'll meet you there."

I'm not sure when *Operation: Buy Lube* became top secret, but I'm having too much fun sneaking around the store with Banner to argue. And besides, I've got a powerful sweet tooth when it comes to ice cream.

"It better not be chocolate," I tell her as I move toward the counter.

The cashier is the slowest in the history of the planet, but since Banner hasn't joined me, I'm not gonna complain.

A small container of Rocky Road lands on the counter next to me.

"I figured Rocky Road was appropriate to pave the way to *brown town*," she says with a laugh.

The man in front of me takes his receipt, and the cashier, a younger woman, reaches for our purchases as soon as Banner starts laughing at her own joke. The cashier's eyes go wide when she comprehends.

"Brown Town? Is that up in the foothills, Logan? I'm not sure I've heard of it," a familiar voice says from behind me.

Oh, for Christ's sake.

I turn around to face Mrs. Harris, her hands full with a box of tea and a bottle of melatonin, but when I open my mouth to respond, nothing comes out.

Banner smiles sweetly and says, "It's just south of Pussy Ridge. At least, I'm pretty sure it is."

I choke, and the cashier's face turns red.

"Pussy Ridge. I haven't heard of that either. I'll have to ask Mr. Harris to get out the Rand McNally so we can take a drive there this weekend. I do love my weekend drives."

I have no idea how Banner is keeping a straight face, but she replies, "I love a good long ride too. Especially when it gets a little rough."

The older woman smiles. "Me too. Emmy has never been a fan, though. She's always gotten carsick at the littlest bump."

Banner finally grins. "That explains so much about her."

The cashier's eyes are tearing up as I shove money at her before I bag the ice cream, Doritos, and lube myself.

"See you later, Mrs. Harris. You'll have to let us know how that drive goes."

I wave, grabbing Banner by the hand and pulling her out of the store behind me. She dissolves into peals of laughter as I open her door and give her a boost into the passenger seat of the truck.

"You're terrible."

Tears are streaming down her face. "What? It was too easy. You have to admit you'd pay to see the look on Mr. Harris's face when she asks him if they can go to Brown Town this weekend."

I cover my face with my hand as my entire body begins to shake. "Jesus, woman. I'll never be able to go into that CVS again without remembering this."

She winks at me. "Good. Mission accomplished."

I shut the door, my lips stretched in a grin as I round the hood to the driver's side.

Nicole comes hurrying out of the store and almost collides with an old man and his walker when she sees me. She jerks in the other direction and hurries off like nothing happened.

What the pharmacy tech said to her comes rolling back through my brain. Pseudoephedrine is used to make meth.

My smile dies away.

Nicole's one of the hardest-working people I know. Always hustling to make extra money because she wants to buy the bowling alley, and everyone knows it.

You can sell a box of over-the-counter drugs with pseudoephedrine in it for good money, from what I've heard around town.

I don't like how things are adding up, especially because I can't think of another reason she'd be maxed out on her limit and trying to buy it three towns away from Gold Haven. Jeff barely escaped from that overdose with his life, and now he's in the county jail awaiting trial because he pled not guilty to distribution, even though the cops found a bunch of shit in his car.

I decide not to say anything to Banner right now. She doesn't have any need to know.

When I climb into my truck and her smile is still intact, I know I'm making the right choice. There's a whole hell of a lot I'd do to keep that shine in her eyes and that laughter on her lips.

"You're fucking beautiful, Banner. But when you laugh, you're the most gorgeous woman I've ever seen."

She quiets, and the smile on her lips fades a few degrees. "You're just saying that because I've got ice cream, and you get to put it in my butt later."

I shake my head. "No. That's not it. You're a damn good woman, and I'm pretty sure you're gonna wreck me for anyone else."

I expect another flippant response, but instead she leans toward me and whispers, "You've already ruined me for other men, so I guess that makes us even."

Right there, in the parking lot of CVS, over ice cream, Doritos, and lube, I realize the truth. I'm in love with her, and I'm totally and completely fucked.

FORTY-ONE

Banner

THE REMAINS OF OUR BINGE LITTER THE TOP OF THE bar. A carton of ice cream, an empty wine bottle, a crumpled bag of Doritos, six empty beers, and an open bottle of lube.

My ass is planted on the counter and my legs are over Logan's shoulders while he proves once again that he does his best work when his hands are involved.

I scream out my orgasm as his fingertips circle the sensitive area just south of my pussy.

"I could tease your ass forever. I can't believe you're finally going to take me here." His words are vibrations against my clit, already rousing the possibility of climax number two.

"If that big cock of yours will even fit."

His finger breaches the muscle and I shiver at the sensation. It's been a while for me, and for some reason, every time feels like the first time when it comes to the back door.

"Your tight little ass is going to be sore tomorrow if I get to fuck you the way I need it."

I don't even care. "You better give me everything you've got."

"Every goddamned inch, baby."

His finger slides in and out, and I arch up to rub my clit against his lips.

Until my phone rings and Logan stops.

"No—"

"Okay."

He keeps going as the ring tone dies away, only to freeze again when it starts back up.

"Seriously! What the hell kind of timing is this?" I screech.

Logan lowers my legs from his shoulders and reaches for my purse with his free hand.

I take it from him, and fish the phone out to check the screen.

Sofia.

I haven't heard from her in days, since she texted an *all is well* update about Myrna.

"Hello?"

"Oh my God, Banner. I didn't know who else to call."

The panic in her voice has me sitting up and closing my legs. "What's going on?"

"She's dead. I just found her. She's dead."

Sofia can only be talking about one person, but for some reason, I have to confirm what I already know as tears sting my eyes. "Myrna?"

She sobs into the phone. "Yes."

"Did you call 911?"

A muffled sound comes next.

"What did you say?"

"They just took her body. Her daughter can't get here until the day after tomorrow. I feel so terrible. She was all alone, sitting in her chair with Jordana right next to her."

I can picture Myrna, and I figure if the old lady was ever going to depart from this Earth, that's probably how she would have wanted it. But even that doesn't stop the grief from welling in my chest.

Logan looks at me, and I can see the question in his eyes.

"What can I do?" I ask Sofia. I lived across the hall from the older woman for five years, and despite all the words we tossed between us, I'm devastated.

"Can you come home? Her daughter told me I need to start organizing things to get rid of, and told me to hire whoever I needed."

"Already? Jesus." It doesn't surprise me as much as it sounds like, however. Mrs. Frances's daughter has barely bothered with her mother in the last five years, so it's not like death is going to change much.

"Yes, and she sounded so heartless. I just . . . I know you had your issues with her—"

Yeah, like she got me evicted. But I can't hold that against her because getting evicted turned out to be one of the best things that ever happened to me.

"I'll be there. It'll be okay. It won't be until tomorrow, though."

"That's fine. I'm going to stay here tonight with Jordana, so she's not alone."

The poor weird little dog. I wonder if Myrna's daughter is going to want to take her. I know for a fact that Sofia's apartment is pet-free, so that's not going to work.

"Okay. I'll call you tomorrow and let you know when I'm in the city."

"Thank you, Banner. I truly didn't know who else to call."

I hang up the phone and see the questions in Logan's eyes.

"What the hell happened? Who died?"

"Mrs. Frances. My old neighbor. The one from across the hall who ratted me out for not having a job."

His brow furrows. "Who interrupted us that first night?"

I nod.

"So you're going to go back to New York for her funeral?"

"I assume I'll be there for the funeral too. I mean, if her daughter even has one."

"Who called you?"

"One of her caretakers. The one who was there the most. Sofia. She's a friend of mine."

"This is the woman who got you evicted, but you're going to run back to New York to help her?"

I release a long breath. "I know it doesn't sound like it makes sense. She was a hard-ass, but she was my hard-ass, you know? I don't think any of it was done in spite. She was . . . kinda like a really strict, bitchy grandmotherly figure to me."

Logan nods like he's trying to understand, but I'm pretty sure he doesn't truly get it. "Okay. You gotta do what feels right."

"I know it seems weird, but this is definitely what's right." Tears trickle over the edges of my lids. "She was crotchety and mean, but she . . . she cared. You know? Like she was the only one who would bother to scold me for coming home late or skipping work. Maybe I'm reaching here, but when you're in a city of a zillion freaking people, that kind of stuff matters. At least, it did to me."

Logan's expression softens as he reaches up to swipe the tears off my cheeks. "Then you go and do what you need to do. Gold Haven will still be here when you get back."

"Thank you for understanding." I straighten my clothes and start looking for a flight on my phone.

Of course, the first one I find is a six a.m. flight out of an airport that's fifty minutes away. I look at Logan, not wanting to ask him to get up at the ass crack of dawn to take me when I know damn well he's got a ton of work to do.

"What?" he asks, looking over at me as he cleans up the mess we made on the counter.

"Is airport parking expensive?" It's not something I've ever had to worry about before.

He gives me a look that clearly says I'm on crack. "Banner, I'm driving you, and I'll pick you up. It's not a big deal."

"I have to be there by five a.m."

"Doesn't matter, babe. We better get back to your place so you can pack."

It's on the tip of my tongue to tell him that I love him, and the words feel so freaking natural, they almost slip out. But I remember my promise to myself, and I lock them down.

"Thank you," I say instead.

He leans in and presses a kiss to my lips. "No thanks necessary."

I fall asleep two hours later with a carry-on packed and Logan wrapped around me in my tiny bed.

I'm going to miss this, even if I'm only gone for a few days. Who would have thought I'd be dreading going back to New York because of what I'm leaving behind in Kentucky?

Namely, my heart.

FORTY-TWO

Logan

I HATE DROPPING HER OFF AT THE AIRPORT. WATCHING Banner walk through those sliding doors, knowing that she's getting on a plane and heading back to a life she could easily want to reclaim, has me tied up in all sorts of knots.

Sure, right now she says she's coming back, but what if she changes her mind? She's not like any woman I've ever met before, and part of what I love about her is her spontaneity and lack of impulse control.

Both those things could easily work against me if she decides that she's had enough of her small-town adventure.

Shit, she wouldn't even need to come back for her clothes; it's not like she left many behind after she was finished packing. How a woman can fit so much stuff in such a small suitcase will forever boggle my mind.

I drive away when the security guard gives me the evil eye. As I turn out of the airport, my phone dings in the cupholder with a text.

Banner NYC: I'm going to miss you.

Right now I'm kicking myself for not changing her contact in my phone to take out the *NYC* because it just hammers home what I'm worried might happen. After having her every day, I can't do the long-distance thing again.

Logan: Not for long.
Banner NYC: xo
Logan: Fly safe.

A car horn honks behind me, and I pull out onto the road toward Gold Haven.

The entire drive, something feels off. I stop at a strip-mall doughnut shop and get some coffee and a half dozen glazed, and leave my phone in the car.

When I get back in the driver's seat, I see another text from Banner on the screen.

Banner NYC: Did I leave my flat iron plugged in upstairs? I seriously can't remember, and if I burn down Holly's gran's house, no one is ever going to forgive me.

Why the woman hadn't just put her hair in a ponytail this morning, I wasn't sure, but I also didn't ask.

Logan: I'll go over there and check before I head home.
Banner NYC: Thank you. Boarding in 15.
Logan: Text me when you land.
Banner NYC: Will do. xo

I eat the entire half dozen glazed doughnuts in less than twenty miles, and finish the coffee before I pull into the gravel drive in front of Banner's temporary home.

Even the word pisses me off. *Temporary.*

She's the first woman who's been in my life in more years than I can count who I don't want the word *temporary* attached to. She doesn't want anything but me. Not my money, not my business, not my house. Just me.

I never have to wonder what the hell she's thinking, or if she's got a hidden agenda, because she's got no filter and has no problem telling me exactly how things are.

That goes a hell of a long way with me.

I head up the steps of the purple porch and use the key Holly gave me to let myself inside. The hallway light is still on, so I'm glad I stopped by regardless. I head upstairs to the bathroom and find the straightener is unplugged. At least Banner will feel better now that she has peace of mind.

But what's shoved in the basket behind it has me freezing where I stand.

The box reads PREGNANCY TEST—TWO PACK. It's torn open and one is missing.

What. The. Fuck.

Logan and Banner's story concludes in *Real Good Love.*

Click on www.meghanmarch.com/#!newsletter/c1uhp to sign up for my newsletter, and never miss another announcement about upcoming projects, new releases, sales, exclusive excerpts, and giveaways.

I'd love to hear what you thought about Banner and Logan's story. If you have a few moments to leave a review on the retailer's site where you purchased the book, I'd be incredibly grateful. Send me a link at meghanmarchbooks@ gmail.com, and I'll thank you with a personal note.

Also by Meghan March

ACKNOWLEDGMENTS

I've never laughed so hard while writing a book. Logan and Banner's story poured out of me, and I hung on for the ride.

Thank you to the amazing team who helped take my words and turn them into a final product of which I'm incredibly proud.

Angela Marshall Smith, the first reader of my words. Your insight is invaluable, and I'm blessed to have you in my life.

Pam Berehulke, editor extraordinaire. Thank you for being so incredibly fabulous in everything you do.

Angela Smith, for taking this crazy ride with me and helping me to keep it all running smoothly. Have I told you lately that I love you?

Danielle Sanchez, publicity goddess. Thank you for handling your job like the boss you are.
Natasha, Jamie, and Stacy, rock-star beta readers. Thank you so much for your feedback and your time. I appreciate it so much more than you know.

Hang Le, amazing cover designer, for once again flexing your creative muscles and delivering exactly what I need.

My Runaway Readers Facebook Group, I feel privileged to have such an amazing crew of ladies and gents who show such passion for my books on a daily basis. Love you all.

My readers, you deserve all the thanks and gratitude I can offer. Without you, I wouldn't have the most amazing job I can possibly imagine. How about we keep doing this thing, yeah?

Fabulous bloggers, for reading and promoting all of these words solely for the love of books. You are the backbone of this indie book world, and don't receive nearly enough credit for all that you do. You are appreciated. You are effing fabulous.

JDW, the epitome of a *real good man*. I could fill an entire book with all the reasons I love you, and am so fucking lucky to have you in my life. I can't wait to see what adventures we're going to have next.

And as always, *my family*, for cheering me on every step of the way.

All my best,
Meghan

AUTHOR'S NOTE

I'd love to hear from you. Connect with me at:

Website: www.meghanmarch.com
Facebook: www.facebook.com/MeghanMarchAuthor
Twitter: www.twitter.com/meghan_march
Instagram: www.instagram.com/meghanmarch

UNAPOLOGETICALLY SEXY ROMANCE

ABOUT THE AUTHOR

Meghan March has been known to wear camo face paint and tromp around in the woods wearing mud-covered boots, all while sporting a perfect manicure. She's also impulsive, easily entertained, and absolutely unapologetic about the fact that she loves to read and write smut.

Her past lives include slinging auto parts, selling lingerie, making custom jewelry, and practicing corporate law. Writing books about dirty-talking alpha males and the strong, sassy women who bring them to their knees is by far the most fabulous job she's ever had.

She loves hearing from her readers at meghanmarchbooks@ gmail.com.

CPSIA information can be obtained
at www.ICGtesting.com
Printed in the USA
LVHW04s0742140818
586741LV00001B/33/P

9 781943 796779